28.

AG LTD 18.

78

CAMERONS CALLING

Books by Jane Duncan

*

CAMERONS CALLING

BY JANE DUNCAN

Illustrated by Victor Ambrus

MACMILLAN
London · Melbourne · Toronto

ST MARTIN'S PRESS
New York
1966

J-62.

MACMILLAN AND COMPANY LIMITED
Little Essex Street London WC 2
also Bombay Calcutta Madras Melbourne

THE MACMILLAN COMPANY OF CANADA LIMITED
70 Bond Street Toronto 2

ST MARTIN'S PRESS INC
175 Fifth Avenue New York NY 10010

Library of Congress Catalog Card Number: 66-16608

PRINTED IN GREAT BRITAIN

Contents

This story is dedicated with respect to
IAN
who knows so much about the Highlands
the saints and the sinners

1. Going on Holiday

'WHAT time is it by your watch, Shona?' Father asked
me as he drove the car into the outskirts of Rioch.
'A minute to three,' I said. 'We'd better hurry or Aunt
will think we aren't coming.'

Father gave a snorting sort of laugh down his nose. '*She*
won't be there,' he said. 'If there is a more unreliable woman
in Scotland than Aunt, I don't want to meet her.'

I felt so astonished that, for a moment, I wondered if I
had heard properly, but when I looked at the side of Father's
face as he drove along, it was wearing an amused and yet
impatient smile as if he were thinking of all the times he had
arranged to meet Aunt somewhere at three in the afternoon
and she had not been there.

'We'll be lucky if we see her before five,' he said.

'I always thought that Aunt was terribly reliable,' I confessed, a little ashamed, for I was nearly sixteen years old at
this time and I felt that it was childish and silly to have
mistaken ideas about someone I knew as well as I thought
I knew Aunt. 'Every time Neil and Donald and I have
travelled up here by train or she had had to meet us anywhere, she has always been there. And that time the aero-

I

plane crashed, she knew exactly what to do and everything.'

'Oh, yes,' Father said, 'she would be reliable with young people like you and Neil and Donald, when she felt responsible, but today, when she knows I am here, she may even forget all about your coming for the holidays.'

'Father!'

'People are different in relation to different people, you see,' Father explained, and he smiled. 'It seems that I have a very bad effect on Aunt. You make her reliable, but I make her unreliable.'

'The minister at Jennyville said Aunt was an amiable eccentric,' my brother Donald said from the back seat. 'What's an amiable eccentric, Father?'

'That old mothball had no right to say any such thing!' said my other brother Neil.

I am the oldest of the family, then comes Neil, who was fourteen at this time, then Donald, who was nine. Our little brother Iain, who was only six, was not with us because Father was taking Neil, Donald and me to spend the summer holidays with Aunt while he, Mother and Iain went on a round of visits to other relations.

'I don't approve of that word "mothball" in that context, Neil,' Father said in his schoolmaster's voice.

'He smells of them,' Neil said, 'and he has no business saying things about Aunt.'

'Father, what *is* an amiable eccentric?' Donald persisted.

'Look it up in the dictionary, Professor,' said Father.

Donald is often called 'the Professor' in the family, partly because he is long-sighted and has to wear spectacles which look out of place on his round face, which is usually fairly dirty, and partly because he is rather clever in a bookish academic sort of way. He is quite different from Neil. Neil has golden-red wavy hair, and a lot of my friends say he is very handsome, although I can never see him looking like anything except my brother Neil Cameron, but it was typical of Neil to be annoyed with the minister for saying that Aunt was an amiable eccentric and to call him an 'old mothball', in spite of knowing that Father would tick him off. It was also typical of Donald to be interested in the words 'amiable eccentric' just for themselves and not to care whether they were complimentary to Aunt or not.

The boys now went back to the books where they were noting the registration numbers of all the cars we passed. Neil was really too old for this game and a bit bored by it, but he was doing it simply to please Donald because he is really a very good-natured boy except when anyone says anything about any of his friends that he regards as insulting. Neil cannot bear anybody to criticise anybody he likes.

'Father,' I asked in a low voice while the boys hustled numbers into their books as the traffic became thicker and thicker as we came nearer to the town, 'would *you* say that Aunt was an amiable eccentric?'

'I suppose I would,' he said. 'She is certainly a very complex character who can be very surprising at times. Yes. Among other things she is an amiable eccentric, but not more so than any of the others up there at Jennyville. They are all eccentrics and all fairly amiable, when you think of it' — he smiled at me secretly and spoke very low — 'even old Mothball the minister.'

He soon turned the car into the Station Square in the middle of Rioch and Neil said: 'Aunt *is* here! There's her car!'

'Aunt and her car are two separate quantities,' Father said.

We all got out and went into the lounge of the Station

Hotel, where we were to meet Aunt. I went round all the corners, looked into all the alcoves and behind all the pillars and then searched in the Ladies' Room, hoping that, for once, Father would be wrong, but he was not, of course. Aunt was nowhere to be seen, but our friend Sandy, who is the porter, left his desk and came over to us.

'Miss Cameron was in town here before breakfast this morning, Mr. Cameron,' he told Father. 'She said to tell you she was at the library, but would be here at three.'

We all looked at the big clock in the corner which said twenty past three and then Father looked back at Sandy.

'Of course,' Sandy said, 'a few minutes this way or that way is neither here nor there, is it? If you will all sit down comfortable, I will tell them to bring you a drop of tea.'

He left us and we all sat down in a mesmerised way.

Rioch is a sort of gateway between the Highlands and the Lowlands of Scotland and every time we come to it from our home in Aberdeenshire, which is in the Lowlands, I get this mesmerised feeling of having passed through a gateway into a land where everything is different in a subtle sort of way that I can hardly describe. For instance, when I thought of what Sandy had said: 'A few minutes this way or that way is neither here nor there, is it?' it simply made no sense at all. Minutes cannot be this way or that way or here or there and yet, when Sandy said that, it seemed to mean that we were making a quite silly fuss about Aunt not being punctual and that we were thinking the face of the clock more important than Aunt enjoying herself in the library.

'The library doesn't close till half past five,' Father said, 'but if she isn't here by five we'll go down there and dig her out.'

'If you are in a hurry to get home, Father,' I said, 'you

can leave us here till Aunt comes. We'll be all right.'

'No. I want to see her. I have a document to sign for her if she has remembered to bring it and, apart from that, I want to see her, anyhow.' He was looking very stern and if we had all been at school instead of in the Station Hotel at Rioch, I would have said that someone was about to have a severe ticking off in Father's study.

'That car of hers is a disgrace,' he said next. 'It looks like a scrap merchant's lorry with all that old rubbish thrown in the back. You two boys had better spend a day cleaning it out for her.'

'Not me!' said Neil.

'Not me either!' said Donald.

Father frowned and Neil explained: 'Last holidays, we got her to take the car down beside the Little River so that we could wash it for her. Then we decided to clean the inside of it as well and—'

'In the back,' Donald continued, 'there was a lot of big old stones and we took them out and threw them in the river—'

'—and it turned out they were geology specimens all full of amethysts and things and she made us put on bathing-trunks and get them out of the river again—'

'—and it was only Easter and there was *ice*!' Donald ended, indignantly.

'So we don't touch that car,' said Neil.

'Camerons calling and repeating:' said Donald, 'we don't touch that car.'

It was not quite five o'clock when Aunt came into the hotel, her hair all flying in wisps, and wearing her old macintosh that has lost its belt and is held together round her middle with a leather luggage strap. And, of course, she was carrying what she calls her handbag, which is really a large leather shopping bag that should zip along the top if only the zipper were not broken and, anyhow, even if the zipper worked the bag is always too full to shut. Her handbag is a bit like that back part of her station wagon and anything may come out of it.

I had never noticed before how terribly untidy Aunt was, but, when I thought of it, it was only in the last few months, since my fifteenth birthday, that I had become interested in clothes and in looking smart. I thought I was looking very well dressed on this day, especially compared with Aunt, for I was wearing my new green sweater and green-and-brown skirt and my new green suede shoes, but after Aunt had said how pleased she was to see us all, she looked at me and said: 'You haven't grown much, Shona. I hope you are not going to turn into a fat little dumpling. And what are you doing with those hideous green shoes on? Don't your feet look big enough without dressing them in that suede stuff? Why don't you wear proper leather shoes? Jock,' she said to Father, 'make her have proper shoes.'

She sat down and then I noticed *her* shoes — brown brogues so polished that they reflected the lights round the walls of the lounge and they seemed to make my new green suede ones look all shabby.

'Liz,' said Father, 'you are two hours late.'

'Am I? Goodness, how time does fly! But you shouldn't have waited. Those three would have been all right here with Sandy.'

'But what about this document to be signed?' Father asked, his voice very short.

'Oh, mercy yes! It's in my handbag. I remembered specially to put it in this morning,' she said, sounding all pleased with herself. She picked up the bag off the floor on to her lap and began to pull things out of it. 'Look at this screwdriver—its absolutely marvellous! Donnie at the garage gave it to me. You just push it against the screw and it goes whirr and the screw is driven. What's this?' She peered into the end of a roll of papers. 'Oh, yes. My notes

about the Strathdonan Stone. And that's a recipe for toffee.
You make it with brown sugar. Tin of shoe polish — wrong
colour — meant to change it. Bit of stag horn. What am I
looking for? Oh, yes. Here it is. You sign it where Mr.
Middleton has put the pencil cross. Sandy,' she called over
to the desk, 'will you and somebody else come and witness
my brother's signature?'

Father signed his name and Sandy and another porter
signed theirs and went away.

'That's one good thing, anyway,' Father said, handing the
paper back to her. 'The Macdonald will be a better tenant
than Gordon ever was.'

At the words 'the Macdonald' I pricked up my ears
because the Macdonald is my very special friend, Somerled
Macdonald of Vannich.

'There was never a good Gordon of Strathdonan,' Aunt
said. 'Father made one of his few mistakes when he leased
the Gordons our land, but they are both dead now and all
that is past.' She put the folded document back in her bag.

'What land, Aunt?' Neil asked. 'Have we got land?'

She smiled. 'Not very much, but we have a little bit.'

'I thought it was just your house and garden, Aunt,' I said.

'No. We have a little more than that. Your father and I
own the land along the shore towards the old fort. It was let
as sheep pasture to Mr. Gordon of Strathdonan, but he died
a few months ago and we have let it to Somerled now.'

'Angus always called Mr. Gordon "Him-Over-There",'
Neil said. 'He was a dirty poacher and a rotter.'

'The man is dead, Neil,' Aunt said. 'We'll let him lie
still in his grave, shall we?' She turned to Father. 'I am
sorry about Strathdonan House, Jock,' she said. 'In principle,
I am in favour of Somerled buying back Macdonald land,

but I wish he would have that house pulled down instead of turning it into a ski lodge.'

'I can't agree with you, Liz,' Father said. 'Glen Vannich and Strathdonan are marvellous for snow, and far safer than the Cairngorms for beginners. Somerled is on to a good thing.'

'Not with that house,' said Aunt obstinately. 'The land is all right, but Strathdonan is an evil house.'

'Oh, you and your spooks!' Father said. 'Look here, Gilliat was on the telephone to me last night.'

'Tim? What about?'

'He has been ringing you at home for the past fortnight and you have never been there.'

'I know. I have been up at Castle Vannich.'

'He has written to you three times, too.'

'Has he? I hardly ever open Tim's letters. They are always about typefaces and things I know nothing about, so there is no point,' said Aunt. 'I just wait for him to get tired and then he publishes my books just the same and does it very well. What did he have to say?'

'What he said was,' said Father, speaking very slowly and distinctly as he does in school when the Latin class is being even more stupid than usual, 'where is that manuscript that you were supposed to have sent him three weeks ago?'

'If *he* doesn't know, how do *I* know?'

'Liz, did you remember to post it?'

'Of course I did. Registered. All plastered with sealing wax the way he likes it.'

'Where is the registration certificate?'

She looked down at the handbag and then began to look uneasy. 'Sandy,' she called after a moment and Sandy came over. 'Sandy, remember that parcel with all the sealing wax that I left with you that day while I went to the Save the Children meeting?'

'Surely I remember it,' said Sandy. 'And if yourself will remember you went to the library and the archives, as they call them, after the meeting and by the time you got back here the post office was closed and myself carried the parcel out and put it in the back of your car, telling you to mind and post it the next day.' He put his head on one side and looked at her solemnly. 'Would you be meaning me to understand that that parcel never got posted after all maybe?'

'I am afraid it didn't, Sandy.'

'Honestly, Liz—' Father burst out in an angry way, but Sandy said: 'Och, now, Mr. Cameron, take a little more tea and do not get excited. We will see to the parcel right away, for it is not yet six o'clock. It may arrive a little behind-hand at where it is going to, but it will be all the same a hundred years after this. Just give me your car keys, Miss Cameron, and I will see to it.'

Aunt gave Sandy the keys and some money to post the parcel and then smiled at Father and said: 'There! If Tim telephones again, you can tell him the parcel was posted right in front of your face. Wasn't it lucky that I forgot all about it until now?'

Father simply stared at her, not saying anything, and then he rose to his feet.

'I am going back home to Inverdaviot,' he said then, 'where I seem to understand things better.' He looked at Neil, Donald and me. 'Have a good holiday you three, and behave yourselves and look after Aunt. She needs it. And keep away from the cliffs at Jennyville.'

'They won't be at Jennyville,' Aunt said. 'We are going straight up to Castle Vannich.'

'Hurrah!' Neil shouted and then clapped his hand over his mouth as everybody in the hotel looked at us.

Father frowned. 'You said you would be at Jennyville for July, Liz!' he said angrily. 'I don't want those three being a nuisance around Somerled's place.'

'I've changed my mind about July and they won't be a nuisance. They will be very useful for August at Castle Vannich too,' Aunt said, and then: 'Jock, you are my favourite brother, being the only one I've got, but I wish you would go away home and stop fussing like an old broody hen.'

Father gave a long sigh. He is very tall, but now he seemed to wilt like a plant that needs water. We three sat staring, for we had never heard anybody speak to Father like this. At school, nobody says anything to him except 'Yes, sir,' and 'No, sir,' and at home he plays games with us and has jokes with Mother, but nobody calls him a 'broody hen'. At last, he merely shook his head wearily and then we went out with him to the car and watched him drive away.

Our luggage was sitting just inside the door of the hotel and Sandy was standing looking at it and scratching his head.

'Is all this forbye yourself and these three to go into that car?' he asked Aunt.

'Of course. We'll manage perfectly,' she told him.

'With the smell and all, that car is going to be what you might call fairly full up,' he said.

'What smell?'

'There is a considerable smell,' said Sandy.

And there was, too. When he opened the doors at the back, a paper bag fell out and burst, and oranges rolled all over the Station Square, but I wondered if 'considerable' was exactly the right word for the smell that came out at the same time.

'Dear me,' Aunt said, 'it's that fish I bought yesterday. I forgot about it. And this is July, after all. Haven't we been having lovely hot weather lately, Sandy?' she asked, handing him a smelly brown-paper parcel.

'Beautiful,' Sandy said, 'just beautiful weather,' holding the parcel out at arm's length to the other porter, who took it and went away, holding his nose between his thumb and his forefinger.

Very soon our luggage and the three of us were crammed into the car and we said good-bye to Sandy, and drove away. We had come from home into Rioch from the south-east and we now drove out of it to the north-west, heading for the hills in central Ross-shire, where Castle Vannich lies. I again had the feeling of having passed through a magic gateway and when the last houses of the suburbs of Rioch had been left behind, I felt that, now, anything could happen, especially something marvellous. We were travelling on the main road to the north which was the usual black ribbon with a white line along the middle and with nothing magic about it, but, on either side of us and especially on our left and to the west, the hills rose higher and higher and looked more and more mysterious, while Ben Vannich, away ahead, stood up against the sky looking very royal and majestic because the evening sun was turning its brown rocks and wine-red bell heather to bright gold and purple.

We were all very quiet, for the boys had the magic feeling too, I think, until we turned a corner and came to a long, straight stretch of road where Aunt began to drive very fast, and Donald, who is always having fits of being dotty about certain things and at this time was dotty about geography, said. 'Aunt, if we went on and on in the direction we are going now, where would we come to?'

'To a watery grave in the Minch, probably,' said Aunt, who was now Aunt as we knew her and not Aunt as Father's elder sister.

'But if we jumped over the Minch?'

'The Outer Hebrides and another watery grave in the Atlantic.'

'But if we jumped over the Atlantic?'

'Iceland,' I said.

'Maybe,' Aunt agreed, 'then another jump and hit the south tip of Greenland.'

'And then?'

'Another jump and it would be the north of Canada — Labrador, perhaps, and then maybe we would be on land for a bit and not have to jump any more.'

The road began to twist again and as Aunt slowed down she said: 'We are having a lot of people from Canada and the United States at the hotel this year. That's why I am spending the whole summer up there.' She made a comic face. 'I have become madly important at the hotel. I even have an office of my own now where I sit at a desk wearing my spectacles and looking brainy.'

'Doing what?' I asked.

She giggled. 'My own work mostly, really, except when anyone wants to know the history of a particular place or interesting places to visit, and then I tell them what I can. But so many of them want to trace their ancestors, and that is nearly impossible with our lack of old records in the Highlands.' She sighed. 'I sometimes get tired of all the enquiries about ancestors.'

Aunt writes books about the Highlands, and I was quite astonished when I got up into senior school to discover that she is quite sort of famous, and more astonished still when

my history master said she was 'a remarkable repository
of Highland lore'. Neil, Donald and I had always known
that she was for ever poking about in libraries and that she
knew far more about the history of the Macdonald of Vannich family than the Macdonalds themselves did, but if you
could see Aunt you would never think of her as famous or
as a repository of anything except junk, like stones with
amethysts in them and parcels of bad fish. However, I was
beginning to think that her mind was rather like her handbag or the back of her car or her house at Jennyville and
simply stuffed with all sorts of things that might come in useful if she kept them for seven years, as she was always saying.

'I can still smell that awful fish in here,' Neil said.

'Aunt,' I asked, 'were you going to keep your fish for
seven years to see if it would come in useful?'

'Ever so smarty-pants, my young niece,' said Aunt, 'laughing at her poor old aunt's bad memory.'

'I am not really laughing, Aunt, not nastily, anyway; and
you certainly haven't got a bad memory. What made you
forget the fish?'

She frowned. 'Strathdonan,' she said.

'Strathdonan? This house you mean?'

'Yes. I had been looking up the history of the Gordons of
Strathdonan and I got so angry that I forgot all about the
fish and everything else.'

'Why?'

'Remember the ruined church on the way to Angus's
house? It was the Gordons who cleared all the crofters out
of that glen and burned their houses down to make way for
the sheep to graze. Our *own* forefathers were some of those
crofters.'

'Angus *said* that Him-Over-There was no good,' said

Neil, who was devoted to our friend Angus and set great
store by everything he ever said.

'The last Mr. Gordon did not do much harm to anybody
as far as I know,' Aunt said, 'but his forefathers were a cruel,
ruthless lot. But it is silly to be angry about people who are
all dead; and stupid of me to let the fish go to waste, but
there it is. It is queer to think of a family coming to a dead
end, isn't it? This man who died was the very last Gordon
of Strathdonan. Just as well, perhaps. It will take most of
what Somerled paid for the house and land to pay his debts,
I am told.'

Donald, although he is the youngest, often seems to be the
most practical of us three, and now he said: 'Aunt, you
said that Somerled was buying back Macdonald land. If it
belonged to the Macdonalds, how did Him-Over-There come
to have Strathdonan?'

Aunt laughed. 'Remember Somerled Macdonald the
Gambler who was killed at Waterloo? Well, the Gambler
lost Strathdonan to a Gordon at a game of cards.'

'Aunt, that's a real tall one!' Neil said.

'Maybe it sounds tall, but it is true. The Macdonalds are
inclined to do everything in a tall way, including gambling.
Well, here we are.'

On our right, across the road, were the north gates of
Castle Vannich which are the main entrance, and on the
gate pillars were little statues of the White Hind, which is
the Macdonald crest. There were thick woods of great old
trees behind the high walls on either side of the gates and
when we went through and past the lodge, going along the
winding drive was like going through a green tunnel where
the evening sun came through the branches only in little
patches, but, after about a mile, the trees gave way to grass

on each side and we went up the last slope to the Great Yett
of the castle while the old black cannon that stood on the
lawn looked down as we approached, like threatening
Cyclops with only one fierce eye, which was the dark mouth
of the barrel.

'What if, suddenly, all the cannon were to fire at us?'
Donald asked.

'I prefer not to think "what if",' Aunt said as she steered
the car into the courtyard.

If you looked at the grass and the flower-beds of the courtyard, it all appeared very gay and rather like a holiday poster,
for the hotel guests were having their drinks out here in the
sunlight before dinner, and the dresses of the ladies were as
bright as the roses in the flower-beds. But if you looked
beyond the people to the great thick walls of the castle and
up at the battlemented top of the old Great Tower, it was
no longer gaily-coloured and shiny like a poster, but rough
and grey and mysterious, and you had a deep, far feeling of
things long ago whose secrets were hidden away among the
stones of these great old walls. To look quickly from the
people, laughing and chatting, to the grey silence of the
building itself was like being in two worlds or two places in
history at the same time and made you feel a little creepy
in a pleasant way.

I was so busy having pleasant creeps that I gave a jump
when a voice said: 'Hello, Shona, you look very smart,'
and found Somerled beside me. I was very pleased that
Somerled thought I looked smart, but could not think of
any answer to make. I thought that Somerled, dressed in his
kilt as usual, looked bigger and handsomer than ever, but I
did not want to say so and, in the end, I said: 'Aunt doesn't
like my shoes because they don't polish.'

'Oh, rot,' said Somerled. 'Your aunt is just an old Highland haybag.'

Donald looked up solemnly through his glasses at Somerled and said: 'People call Aunt a lot of very interesting things. If I were to collect them all in a notebook, could it be sold for lots of money at Sotheby's after she is dead?'

'No, it couldn't, you morbid mercenary little brute,' said Aunt, handing him his bag. 'Here. Carry that up to your room. Neil, here is yours. Same rooms as last year.'

'Is Angus here?' Neil asked.

'Yes. Somewhere about,' said Somerled, taking my bag and some of Aunt's things and we all went inside and up the main staircase and on up the winding corkscrew stairs to our rooms on the top floor of the south front, which looks out over Loch Vannich.

It was pleasant to come again into the room that I had first seen the summer before, when the castle was just in process of being turned into an hotel and I felt that I was being given a special welcome when I looked at the painting of the White Hind of Vannich that hung above the stone fireplace. The painting is very beautiful and while I was looking at it Somerled put my case down on the seat at the window and said: 'But wait till you see what we have done in the wall of the Tower, Shona. Your aunt had a brilliant idea. Sometimes she is almost a genius, I think.'

'You take back what you said about a Highland haybag?' Aunt asked, coming in.

'You can be a Highland haybag and almost a genius too,' Somerled told her, 'but never mind. We all love you, don't we, Shona?'

I only smiled, but Aunt laughed and said: 'Then love us enough, Somerled, to leave us alone to get tidy for dinner.'

'I go at once,' said Somerled, making a deep bow, and, when the door had closed behind him, Aunt said: 'One wants to take a firm line against the blandishments of these Macdonalds.'

'You know a lot about the Macdonalds, don't you, Aunt?' I asked.

She shrugged her shoulders. 'I know enough to beware of their golden-haired charm,' she said and went away to her own room.

2. Camerons Calling from Canada

SOMERLED was about twenty-five years old, his mother and father were dead and he had no relations except for two aunts and some very distant cousins. His aunts, Miss Dorothy and Miss Constance Macdonald, lived with him at Castle Vannich and were known to everybody as Miss Dotty and Miss Coocoo, which was quite a good description of them. Miss Dotty bred gun dogs which were supposed to be for sale, but she grew so fond of them all that she never sold any, and the kennels simply grew bigger and bigger and fuller and fuller. Miss Coocoo bred budgerigars which were supposed to be for sale, but she grew so fond of them all that she never sold any, and her aviary had expanded until it filled two large rooms in the west front. Miss Dotty was tall and dark and hardly ever spoke, and Miss Coocoo was small with silver curls and hardly ever stopped talking in a fluttery cooing voice but, although they were so different, they both had this Macdonald charm that Aunt had mentioned, so that, although they were always making muddles and getting in everybody's way, everybody was very fond of them.

When the three of us and Aunt came down to breakfast on the first morning, we met Miss Dotty and Miss Coocoo in the hall, and Miss Coocoo hugged us all — even Neil does not mind being hugged by Miss Coocoo — and said: 'But *where* is that *dear* little Iain boy with the red hair? You *haven't* gone and lost him *again* have you?'

'I told you only yesterday that Iain wasn't coming this year, Coocoo,' Aunt said.

'You told me no such *thing*, did she Dotty? And if you *did*, I didn't *believe* you, I *am* disappointed. I was *so* looking forward to *seeing* him, don't you know?'

'Bah!' Miss Dotty said scornfully, looking at Neil, Donald and me as if we did not at all make up to her for the absence of Iain.

'We are looking forward to seeing the dogs and the budgerigars,' Neil said, being tactful and changing the subject, which one has to do all the time with Miss Dotty and Miss Coocoo.

'We will not be speaking of dogs or of budgerigars either, just for the present,' said our friend Angus, coming down the stairs.

'Come and have breakfast.'

Miss Dotty and Miss Coocoo melted away — they have a way of simply disappearing that is a little like the Cheshire Cat in *Alice* — and we went with Angus into the dining-room.

'Why mustn't we speak about the dogs and the budgerigars?' Neil asked Angus when we were at table, annoyed that his tact had failed. 'Last year, Miss Dotty and Miss Coocoo didn't want ever to talk about anything else.'

'Times have changed, as times have a way of doing,' Angus told him.

Angus is Somerled's head shepherd, but he does not do much work with the sheep any more. Somerled calls him his guide, philosopher and friend, and this is a good description of him because he can guide you all over the Vannich Estate; he is as wise as a philosopher; and he is a terrific friend of all of us. He is very old, although none of us know his age. He was a soldier in the service of Queen Victoria and he can remember the earliest telephones and the earliest motor-cars. He is thin and spry and has a short, pointed beard which, along with his bright, wise, old eyes, makes him look a little like a wise old gnome who might live in some cave in the rocky side of Ben Vannich. Actually, when he is not at the castle, he lives in a fascinating house at the foot of the Ben, a house which is full of Willow Pattern china, all sorts of curiosities and has an air of magic.

'We ran into a little difficulty with the dogs and budgerigars,' he said now. 'As was natural, many of the visitors who came here wanted to buy them and for a time it looked as if we were going to make our fortunes with them.'

'But what went wrong?' Neil asked.

'As was natural, Miss Dorothy and Miss Constance did not want to sell either dogs or birds, so they have now given them all away to their friends except for a pair of each which they have kept for themselves.'

'Gave them away?' Donald asked, blinking through his glasses.

'Just that. Miss Dorothy and Miss Constance enjoy giving things to their friends, but they do not enjoy selling things to strangers — things they are fond of, that is — and it is only reasonable that the ladies should be allowed to enjoy themselves in their own way. But now that we have got over the little difficulty of the dogs and the birds, they are very happy with their tartan cushions.'

'Tartan cushions?' I asked, feeling, as I often did when I listened to Angus talking about the Macdonald family, that the world was being turned inside out and me along with it.

'Yes. They are making cushions in tartan patchwork,' said Angus. 'They do not like to sew, they do not like tartan cushions and they do not like patchwork, so, when they have made them, they enjoy selling them to the visitors, who buy them in ever-increasing numbers. Please to pass me over a scone, Neil.'

'Yes, Shona,' Aunt said. 'I meant to warn you. If Miss Dotty or Miss Coocoo shows you one of their cushions, don't admire it, remember. Say: "Goodness, how hideous!" or something like that.'

At that moment, Miss Dotty and Miss Coocoo came into the room and over to our table, each carrying a cushion made of hexagonal pieces of different tartans all sewn together, and displayed them to us.

'Mercy!' said Angus, 'that one is the ugliest I have seen yet, Miss Constance, and I am not sure that Miss Dorothy's is not even worse.'

'Terrible!' said Aunt.

'Goodness, how hideous!' I said.

'They make my eyes feel sick,' said Donald.

'You can't take money for *these*!' Neil said dramatically in a horrified voice and the ladies looked absolutely delighted with themselves.

'Oh, yes we *can*!' said Miss Coocoo. 'Three guineas *each*! Isn't it *fun*?'

'Bah!' said Miss Dotty and looked down with loathing at the cushion between her hands.

'After breakfast, Shona,' Miss Coocoo said, 'you *must* come and help us to cut *patches*. It is *most* satisfying, cutting up yards and *yards* of tartan into these horrid little square circles.'

She turned to Aunt. 'Dotty and I have stopped doing the *sewing* part — too dull and boring and the thread getting in *knots* all the time. Mrs. Elton and some of the others are doing it for us. *We* just cut out the square circles and then *sell* the horrible things. *Such* fun! And Mrs. Elton can make them *much* more hideous than we could. *She* made *these*,' she ended with pride.

'She is certainly a master at it,' said Aunt.

When we all had said again how hideous the cushions were, Miss Dotty and Miss Coocoo went away, and I said to Aunt: 'I don't really understand. These cushions are not really so very hideous.'

'Dotty and Coocoo think they are and that's all that matters,' Aunt said.

'Angus,' Donald asked, 'are Miss Dotty and Miss Coocoo amiable eccentrics?'

'An eccentric thing or person, I understand,' Angus said, 'is something or some person whose centre is not in the middle, but the thing that puzzles me is where exactly the middle is. It is possible, Donald, that *your* centre is not in the middle and Miss Dorothy's and Miss Constance's are dead on the bull's eye.'

'Or maybe everybody has a different middle,' Aunt said.

Neil put his thumbs in his ears, waggled his fingers and made a whooping noise like a Red Indian and I was feeling like doing it too when Somerled came into the room and over to us with an open telegram in his hand and a frown on his face.

'Another communication from your rich relations,' he said to Aunt, putting the paper between her and me on the table.

'Evan Cameron Third and party arrive five o'clock today Saturday,' it said.

'Well, now we know,' said Aunt.

'I'm sick to death of this lot,' said Somerled. 'Angus, let's you and I get into the Land-Rover and go over to Strathdonan.'

'Somerled,' Aunt said, 'I don't think you can do that. I think you should be here to welcome this Cameron party.'

Somerled glared at her. In the ground-floor room of the Great Tower, there is a portrait of a very fierce ancestor of Somerled's who was known as Somerled the Red and the present-day Somerled seemed to be looking more like him every moment.

'Look here,' he said, frowning down at Aunt, 'this Cameron may be the richest man in Canada and all that, but that is no reason why *I* should lick-spittle around his heels. I've had more than enough of him. First of all, they are coming by air and then they change their minds and come by sea and are a fortnight late. Then they have to have a suite on the ground floor, so we fix them up a suite on the ground floor. Then they have to have accommodation for two chauffeurs, so we make accommodation for two chauffeurs. Then they have to have an electric typewriter and two telephones connected direct to the exchange at Rioch in the ground-floor suite. And now *you* are saying that I have to dance the Highland Fling in the courtyard when they condescend to arrive this afternoon.'

'I am saying nothing of the sort,' said Aunt. 'All I am saying is that if you set out to keep an hotel, you should do the job properly. These people have booked seven bedrooms and a sitting-room for eight weeks, they have paid half the fee in advance, and it is our job to be civil to them.'

'Elizabeth is speaking sense, Macdonald,' Angus said quietly.

'Oh, all right.' Somerled was surly. 'But don't blame *me* if things go wrong. I have a sort of foreboding about Emperor Evan Cameron the Third. I feel that he and I are not going to get along—Who is for a run across the loch in the motor-boat?'

The boys and Angus went away with Somerled and I said to Aunt: 'Are these people who are coming really relations of ours?'

'No,' she said. 'They happen to have the same surname, that's all.' She picked up the telegram and sighed. 'Somerled has been difficult about them from the very outset. They are stinking rich and I must admit that they send very arrogant cables and telegrams, as if the whole world existed for nothing except to serve them. And Somerled is pretty arrogant himself. But if you are running an hotel, you are running an hotel and Somerled must be made to remember it. Actually, it is not easy for him and he is very good about it most of the time.'

Castle Vannich did not look much like an hotel. While Aunt went off to her office, I went all around the ground floor, visiting my friends in the kitchens and the laundry. It was like wandering through a very large private house, for there was no hall with a reception desk and a porter's desk like the hall of the Station Hotel in Rioch. When people arrived, the receptionist came out of her office and into the ground-floor part of the Great Tower, bringing the registration book with her and, after the names had been filled in, the people were just like guests visiting friends in a private house.

When I had seen everybody in the kitchens and laundry, I crossed the courtyard to visit the waitresses in the tea-room on the west front. This room was for people who came only to visit the gardens and the museum in the dungeons and who were not staying in the hotel and it was staffed mostly with girls only a little older than myself, high-school girls and university and art-school students who worked here in the summer vacation. They were a very gay crowd and looked very smart and pretty, for they all wore white blouses, tweed skirts and little caps and aprons of Vannich Macdonald tartan. But today, when I went in, they were not gay. They were all crowded round one girl, called Bessie, who was lying on the floor among a lot of broken china and crying with pain.

'It's my ankle,' she kept sobbing, 'my ankle!'

'I'll get Aunt,' I said and ran away.

When two of the waiters had carried Bessie away to the dormitory and the doctor had been sent for and all the fuss was over, Aunt said: 'Shona, you had better go to Miss Smiley and get a cap and apron and take Bessie's place until we get another girl out from Rioch.'

As Aunt had said, if you are running an hotel, you are running an hotel. Neil, Donald, Iain and I had a share of ten pounds each in Castle Vannich Limited and this was a Saturday in the height of the summer season and so there it was. I went to Miss Smiley, the manageress's, room and came out dressed in a tartan cap and apron.

As a matter of fact, being a waitress in the tea-room is enormous fun. I had had a go at it the year before and most of the people who come in for morning coffee or afternoon

tea are very pleasant and friendly. They are also very
generous in the matter of tips.

Very soon, the first bus-load arrived and after that we
were rushing about like crazy until it was lunch-time and,
instead of joining Aunt and the boys for lunch, I went to
the staff-room with the others and joined the big noisy party
of gardeners, laundry people and the boys who were the
guides in the museum. Then, by three o'clock, the tea rush
had begun and we all careered about again, but towards five
o'clock the hustle was over and we all gathered in a corner
by the window to count our tips.

Through the window I saw Somerled, Angus, Neil and
Donald sitting on the Stirrup Stone in the courtyard, Angus
in his hairy tweed suit and my brothers dressed in the kilt
and white shirt like Somerled, who was looking very cross
and angry, and then I remembered about Evan Cameron
the Third, so I left the tea-room and went out to find Aunt,
Miss Dotty, Miss Coocoo and the receptionist all waiting in
the ground floor of the Great Tower.

Aunt smiled. 'Full parade,' she said, 'but I *do* wish
that Somerled could look more welcoming and less war-
like.'

At that moment, two huge shiny cars swept through the
arch of the Great Yett, and Somerled, the boys and Angus
rose to their feet from the Stirrup Stone.

Somehow, an excitement had come into the air as if an
emperor were indeed arriving. All the waitresses and Miss
Smiley were in a covey at the door of the tea-room and I
could see the kitchen people crowded at the windows, so it
was a little flat when the first car stopped, the chauffeur got
out and opened the door with his other hand at the peak of
his cap and a little, wizened-up, rheumaticky old man was

c

helped out by two other men and given a walking-stick on which he leaned as he peered round at the castle walls like a short-sighted angry old tortoise. Then a boy of about my age got out of the car and a lady and gentleman got out of the other one. The old gentleman pointed up at the Great Tower with his stick. 'Well,' he said, 'the people that built that could certainly build.'

'Get Somerled over here,' Aunt whispered to me and stepped forward towards the old man with her hand held out.

It was all very well, I thought, as I ran towards the Stirrup Stone, for Aunt to say: 'Get Somerled.' The way Somerled was looking at these two cars and all the people fussing round the old man, I felt it might be easier to dig up Ben Vannich and carry it into the Great Tower in a bucket.

'Somerled, Aunt says to come, please,' I said in a shaky voice.

Angus was looking across at the old gentleman with the stick. 'Poor old man,' he said quietly and Somerled suddenly smiled. 'All right, Shona,' he said. 'Actually, the emperor isn't what I had expected at all.'

When Somerled, Angus, Neil, Donald and I came into the Great Tower, Aunt had introduced herself and was now being introduced by the old gentleman to the rest of his party, who were his son, Evan Cameron the Fourth and his wife, his grandson, Evan Cameron the Fifth and the two other gentlemen who were secretaries.

'And here, Mr. Cameron,' said Aunt, 'is the owner of the hotel, the Macdonald of Vannich.'

The little old gentleman looked up at Somerled's face, then right down to his feet and up to his face again. He then looked up at the painting of Somerled the Red on the wall and back to the present-day Somerled before he pointed at the painting with the stick and said: 'That a forebear of yours?'

'Yes, sir,' said Somerled quietly, but I knew that he was once more very angry.

'I didn't expect to run up against *you*,' old Mr. Cameron said. 'In my book you are the latest one of a bad lot.'

'Now, Father—' the second Mr. Cameron was beginning when Somerled, his eyes looking like blue jewels with red lights in them, turned to Aunt: 'Miss Cameron,' he said, 'please arrange for this party to leave tomorrow morning,' and without another word, he went out through the door, Angus, Neil and Donald following him.

The old Mr. Cameron seemed to shrivel up into a little ball of rage. He shook his stick at Somerled's back and seemed to be going to have a fit of some sort while all his party fussed around, trying to make him calm, which only made him angrier than ever. He began to rave about how Somerled's ancestors had burned down his great-grandfather's house and all the other houses and how the people of the glen were all scattered and his own grandfather ended up in Canada; but, at last, speaking very loudly, Aunt made him stop and listen to her.

'Mr. Cameron,' she almost shouted, 'you are making a dreadful mistake. My name is Cameron, too, and I can assure you that the Macdonalds of Vannich never evicted any crofters or burned any houses!'

At last the old gentleman became quiet and we sat him down in an armchair and I had to fetch a glass of water so that they could give him a pill.

'All right,' he then said fiercely to Aunt, 'you talk and I'll listen, but you will have to do some good talking to get over the evidence I have in the car out there.' He pointed the stick at one of the secretaries. 'You, there, go and get that private case of mine.'

When the man came back with a small leather case, Mr. Cameron took it on his knees, unlocked it and took out a big old bible and, looking up at Aunt, he said: 'This is my great-grandfather's bible and that is his handwriting. Read it.'

I stood by Aunt's elbow and read the faded writing too: 'Let all my children and my children's children remember that the graves of their forebears and their rightful home are in the broad Glen that lies in the shadow of Ben Vannich. Let them never forget the injustice of this day. Evan Cameron, Stone Mason. May 1804.'

'All right,' the old man barked at Aunt as he closed the big book, 'talk.'

'Your great-grandfather, Mr. Cameron,' Aunt said, 'was evicted from Glen Vannich by a man called Gordon. I can prove it and I can show you a letter of protest that was sent to him by the Macdonald of Vannich of that time. The letter is here because Gordon sent it back to the Macdonald with a pen stroke drawn through it. You will see it for yourself later.' She drew a deep breath and looked round at the whole party before she said: 'Mr. Cameron, you owe the Macdonald an apology.'

'Me? Apologise to that young whippersnapper? I've never apologised to anybody in my life!'

I thought he was going to have another fit, but Aunt looked very tall and stern as she said: 'There is a first time for everything, Mr. Cameron. You heard the order I was given. If you do not apologise, you will not be accepted as a guest.'

'Not accepted?' He raised the stick and shook it. 'I'll sue you! I'll—'

'Now, Father—'

'Please, sir—' they all began at once, but Aunt walked out of the room and I followed her. I felt all shaky, and my voice trembled as I said: 'Oh, goodness, Aunt!'

'It's all right, Shona. He is simply a very arrogant old gentleman who has had all his own way all his life and now he has a bad heart as well. He will calm down. At least, I hope so.'

We went over to the Stirrup Stone, where Somerled was standing with a face like thunder, Angus looking very calm and wise and Neil and Donald looking rather scared, like me. We had never seen people so furiously angry before—not grown-up people, at least.

Somerled glared at Aunt. 'I told you I had a feeling in my bones about that lot!' he said.

'Now, listen, Somerled,' she began, and as she talked the red light died out of his blue eyes. 'And I believe he will toe the line,' she ended. 'He is an old man, Somerled, and sick, and he is full of old bitter memories. He may not make a very good job of apologising, this being his first shot at it, but you must accept his apology all the same. It was all a ridiculous mistake, anyhow.'

'Yes, Macdonald,' Angus said, 'do not hold the old man's mistake against him.'

Old Mr. Cameron appeared in the doorway of the Great Tower, pointed his stick at Somerled, and shouted: 'You there! Come here!' He might have been calling to a dog that he did not like very much and when Somerled glared across the courtyard at him I did not know whether to feel scared again or to laugh, because the old man looked like anything rather than somebody who felt apologetic. But when Somerled did not move, he pointed his stick at me and called in a much kinder voice: 'Little girl, come here.'

'Go to him, Shona,' Aunt said.

Feeling rather nervous, I set off across the courtyard, but his wrinkled-up old face was really quite pleasant when he leaned on his stick, looked down at me and said: 'Will you tell that young man that I am not very well and can't walk much? Will you tell him I am sorry I insulted him and would like to shake hands with him?'

I went back to Somerled and repeated the words and then I said: 'Do go, Somerled. He is really sorry and it was all a mistake.'

Somerled did not say anything. He simply walked across and held out his hand to the old man.

After that, we all had a very pleasant chat together except that, because I was still wearing my tea-room cap and apron,

Mr. Cameron made up his mind that I was one of the maids and that he wanted me as his private maid to bring all his meals to his sitting-room. When Mr. Cameron made up his mind about anything, it was very difficult to unmake it, so that, in the end, it was simpler, as Aunt said, for me to take on the holiday job of being personal maid to him. It was very odd, because he knew perfectly well that I was Aunt's niece and at the castle on holiday, but he did not want to know this because, having apologised to Somerled, he wanted to have entirely his own way about something else that Somerled did not approve of.

'It is just that he is cranky,' Angus explained, 'and likes to have all his own way, poor old man.'

'He's not as old as you are,' Somerled said huffily.

'I will give you that maybe he is not as old as I am in years,' Angus said, 'but he is a lot older in foolishness. I am old in years maybe but not foolish enough yet to believe that anybody can have all his own way.'

'Well, I like him,' I said, 'and I can easily carry his trays in.'

'And I bet he'll give you a whopper of a tip at the end of the holidays,' Donald said, 'lucky you. Aunt, couldn't I get a cap and apron too?' And everybody laughed. 'Aunt, is Mr. Cameron an amiable eccentric?'

'I suppose he is as eccentric as the rest of us,' Aunt said, 'and more amiable now than he was to start with.'

Mr. Cameron invited Aunt to have dinner with him in his sitting-room and as I went in and out with the food, I overheard that they were talking all the time about the Highland Clearances. This is one of those little bits of history that suddenly come alive when you see the valley of the River Vannich, just like so much that happened long ago comes alive when you visit a place like Edinburgh Castle or the Tower of London. In lower Glen Vannich there stands the ruin of a church and nothing else except broad acres of pasture where hundreds of sheep graze, but in 1800 there was a whole township of little houses with a few acres of cultivated land round each of them. It was in 1804 that the Mr. Gordon who had won Strathdonan from Somerled Macdonald the Gambler 'cleared' this glen, the 'clearance' being the eviction of the people and the burning or pulling down of their houses so that the land could be put under grass for the sheep to eat, because Mr. Gordon could make more money out of sheep than he could make out of people. People, as Aunt told Neil, Donald and me when we first saw the ruined church, do not grow wool which can be made into cloth and sold for money and they cannot be slaughtered and eaten as mutton, so Mr. Gordon 'cleared' the people off his land. This was a thing that happened in many parts of the Highlands, the most notorious of all being the Sutherland Clearances, but Aunt has made something of a special study of the Vannich Clearances, and old Mr. Cameron was tremendously interested in all she could tell him and, after I took in their coffee, they went on talking and Aunt told me to chase Neil and Donald off upstairs.

I was going up to our rooms with my brothers, but Mr. Cameron's son and his wife stopped me at the foot of the stairs to thank me for humouring old Mr. Cameron, as they called it. Somerled and Angus were there, too, and Mrs. Cameron said to them: 'It sounds crazy, but I believe it was this Glen Vannich business that brought on his first heart attack.'

'It's not so crazy,' Mr. Cameron said. 'Ever since I can remember, he has talked of visiting Glen Vannich some day, but it never happened. He was always too busy making money, I guess. Then, he retired from business and quite by chance he saw an advertisement for your hotel here in some magazine. He showed it to me and he kept saying: "Castle Vannich Hotel — *Vannich*!" and I noticed that his hand was shaking. You know, I don't think Vannich was a real place to him till he saw that publicity in cold print. Before that, Vannich was a sort of fairy-tale place that he had heard his father and grandfather talk about when he was a kid. Anyways, there it was. He got all steamed up and decided on this trip and then he had the heart attack, but nothing would stop him. That was when we had to cable you about the ground-floor suite.' Mr. Cameron smiled. 'As you may have noticed, Dad takes a lot of stopping once he makes up his mind, and I am certainly grateful to you people for the way you have handled him. I hope he doesn't keep your Aunt in there all night,' he added to me.

'Aunt is enjoying herself,' I told him. 'They are talking about the Clearances and Aunt would talk about that till the cows come home.'

However, Aunt came upstairs before we were asleep. I was in the boys' room, having a chat and sharing Donald's bed to keep warm and she came in and sat down on the end of Neil's bed.

'Did the Third have any more fits?' Neil asked.

'No. He is rather charming, really, isn't he, Shona?'

'Yes. I've been telling Neil and Donald he is a bit like Angus in a way, but scratchy instead of smooth like Angus.'

Aunt smiled. 'He is absolutely hipped on the Clearances,' she said. 'I know you lot think I'm pretty hipped on them myself, but with me it is more a sort of curiosity because there is so little reliable first-hand evidence about them, especially the Vannich Clearances. That old bible of his is one of the most fascinating items I have seen.' She got up and went to look out of the window into the cold gilt light of the late evening. '—visiting the iniquity of the fathers upon the children unto the third and fourth generation—' she quoted. 'The Clearances were an iniquity, but when in 1804 Evan Cameron wrote in his bible: "Let them never forget the injustice of this day", that was an iniquity too. It led to that old man coming here today full of hatred and spite.' She turned round and smiled at us. 'We must do everything we can to make him change his mind.'

'And not have any more fits,' said Donald.

'No. The fits are bad for him, but I rather think the spite and hatred are even worse,' she said. 'All right. Bed now. Tomorrow is another day.'

3. *A House with a Shadow*

THE next day Somerled and old Mr. Cameron were the
best of friends. Like most of the other people who came
to the castle, Mr. Cameron was very interested in what Neil,
Donald and I call 'the Somerleds', which are all the paintings
of Somerled's ancestors which hang around the walls. All
the people in the portraits are not called Somerled, of course,
but many of them are and most of them have nicknames like
Somerled the Red, Somerled the Scholar and Somerled the
Locksmith. However, there are quite a few Neils and Simons
among them, and some Harriets, Dorothys and Constances
too.

The most important paintings, from the point of view of
visitors to the castle, hang in the ground-floor room of the
Great Tower, and the four main ones are Somerled the Red,

because he was the earliest one to be painted, Somerled the Hotel-keeper, who is the Somerled I know and the latest one to be painted, and Somerled the Gambler and Charles the Sailor, because the last two pictures are very valuable, being the work of the famous artist Raeburn.

But Mr. Cameron was most interested in the picture of Somerled the Gambler, who was the one who gambled away the lands and house of Strathdonan and thus led indirectly to Mr. Cameron's forefathers being evicted from their croft and having to seek their fortunes in Canada. There are several portraits of Somerled the Gambler, although only one by Raeburn and I think he must have been a very vain gentleman who was well aware how good-looking he was. The Raeburn portrait shows only his head and shoulders, a very handsome face under bright red-gold hair, but there is another full-length picture of him, very richly dressed in the style of Beau Brummel, standing by a table, holding a Knave of Hearts in his hand and looking very reckless and very pleased with himself.

'Be things as they may,' old Mr. Cameron said, looking at this one, 'he was a handsome rascal.'

'He was certainly a rascal,' Aunt said.

'Well, now,' said Angus in his slow, quiet way, 'who is to say where rascaldom begins and ends?' Angus often uses fascinating words like 'rascaldom' which he makes up himself. 'The Gambler was a brave man as well as a bonnie one and to be both brave and bonnie excuses a lot, I am thinking.'

Angus, you see, feels about the Macdonald family as Neil feels about Angus. Angus can see no flaw in any Macdonald and Neil can see no flaw in Angus. Mark you, I have to admit that Angus is pretty flawless.

'Did any of the rest of them gamble?' Mr. Cameron asked.

'None to the extent that the Gambler did,' Aunt answered, 'until the present day,' and she looked at Somerled, 'when this one gambled the castle and the whole estate, double or nothing.'

'What?' Mr. Cameron swung round and glared at Somerled out of his fierce old eyes.

'When he undertook this hotel venture,' Aunt explained, 'it really was a desperate throw, all or nothing, but it does look as if he is going to win,' and she smiled.

'Good for you, young fellah,' said old Mr. Cameron and then went on: 'I was asking if gambling ran in the blood because it is one of my beliefs that people can inherit other things besides the colour of their hair from their forebears. As you may know, my firm is the Cameron Construction Company of Canada —'

'It's more of an empire than a firm, really, isn't it, sir?' Somerled asked.

'Maybe. I'll grant you it is quite a firm, anyways. But it all began with my grandfather, Evan Cameron, a stone-mason like his father before him. Nowadays, of course, we go in for a lot of steel and concrete construction, but there isn't one of us Camerons who can't build this way' — he pointed with his stick to the rough stone walls of the Great Tower — 'with rough stone and our bare hands. Even my grandson, Fifth there, has built a wall in the garden at home.'

When he referred to his grandson, the boy of about my age as 'Fifth' I suddenly thought that there had probably been as many Evan Camerons as there had been Somerled Macdonalds and I said: 'Your grandson is not really only the Fifth is he? He must be about the umpteenth, just like Somerled.'

The old man smiled at me, looking pleased. 'Maybe,' he said, 'but we lost track when we lost our home in Glen Vannich and we did not start to number ourselves until I was old enough to join the firm. There was my grandfather, there was my father, who was called Evan Cameron Junior, and so they had to call me the Third so that people would know which one they were talking about.' He turned to Aunt and Somerled. 'I got good and mad when you wrote me that first letter that started "Dear Mr. Third,"' he said. 'Darn it, I thought, what sort of outfit do they think they are over there?'

'We are very sorry about that,' Aunt said smiling 'but we actually had a man called Robert Third staying here last year and we thought you were one of the same clan when your first cable came in.' She glanced at Somerled. 'There were a few times in the course of our correspondence with you when we got good and mad too, you know.'

'Folks often get mad at the things I say and the letters I write,' Mr. Cameron said. 'I don't know why it is. But, anyways, we are not mad at each other any more and I would take it as a great favour if you could arrange with the owners of this Strathdonan place for me to make an excursion there. Don't get me wrong. I don't want to meet these Gordons or whoever they are or take tea with them or anything, but I would sure like to see this glen that's mentioned in my great-grandfather's bible.'

'There are no Gordons of that family left to take tea with,' Aunt told him. 'The last of them died seven months ago. It will be easy to arrange an excursion for you because'— she indicated Somerled—'this modern-day gambler has just bought Strathdonan back from the executors of the Gordon Estate.'

'Well,' the old man looked with approval at Somerled, 'if that isn't something!'

'I'm not so sure, sir,' Somerled said. 'I'd like your opinion because I've gone against the advice of my two best advisors, Miss Cameron and Angus here, in buying Strathdonan.'

'Oh?' Mr. Cameron pulled down his fierce eyebrows. 'Well? Go on.'

'When we opened the castle here as an hotel last year,' Somerled said, 'we thought it would be only a summer thing and maybe a little while at Christmas, but it isn't. People have come all the year round and we had terrific snow last winter, but we couldn't give them ski-ing because the Vannich Estate is mostly woodland, apart from the Ben itself, that is. Then Strathdonan and the Broad Glen of Vannich came on to the market when Gordon died and I bought the lot. The idea is a ski-centre, sir.'

'Sounds like a proposition to me,' Mr. Cameron said and looked at Aunt and Angus. 'What have you against it?'

They now looked at one another and then down at the floor until Mr. Cameron became impatient, which did not take very long, thumped on the floor with his stick and said: 'You been struck dumb, for Pete's sake?'

Angus looked up at him and said: 'Strathdonan is a bad house. No good can come of it.'

'Yes,' Aunt said, taking courage from Angus. 'Bad will come of it before good. It is an evil house. It ought to be pulled down.'

Mr. Cameron looked at them, getting angrier every second, and then: 'What d'you mean by a *bad* house, an *evil* house? Insanitary, you mean? Old? Unsoundly built? What?'

Aunt glared at him, seemingly as angry as he was. 'No,'

she said. 'Nothing like that. It is a wicked house, so wicked that it is haunted!'

'Haunted? Do you mean ghosts, for Pete's sake?'

'Yes,' said Aunt defiantly. 'Ghosts or worse!'

'Now, look here, Miss Cameron,' he said, thumping the floor with his stick, 'you are a well-read sensible woman. Are you standing there telling me that you believe in ghosts?'

'I am telling you that Strathdonan is an evil house,' she said.

'And badness has been done there,' Angus added, 'and where badness has been done and never regretted and never forgotten and never forgiven, badness lives on.'

'Badness fiddle-faddle!' Mr. Cameron turned to Somerled. 'Young fellah, where is this place? You let me see it. I'll soon tell you whether it'll make a ski lodge or not and if it will, my son will set up the plans for you and save you hiring an architect. If the building is sound, we'll make a ski lodge of it and—' he glared at Aunt and Angus '—no badness or ghosts will stop us! Ghosts, for the love of Pete!' He shook his stick above his head. 'Did I come all the way from Toronto to be scared off by a ghost?' And with this he went creaking and jerking out into the courtyard in his impatient way, with Somerled following behind him.

When Mr. Cameron wanted to do anything, he did not want to do it tomorrow or even in a short time, he wanted to do it that very moment.

'Indeed,' Angus said, 'he would like to go to Strathdonan the day before yesterday if that was not impossible.'

So, this being a Sunday and there being no new arrivals expected that afternoon, it was decided that we would make an expedition to Strathdonan immediately after lunch: Mr. Cameron, his grandson Fifth, Aunt and I in one car and

Somerled driving Angus, Neil and Donald. Aunt did not really want to go, but Mr. Cameron wanted her to answer all his questions about the district, and I went because Neil and Donald were going, and Angus went because Somerled was going. I sat in front with Fifth and the chauffeur, and Fifth was very interesting about his home in Canada, his two younger sisters and the school he went to, but, like most boys, Neil and Donald included, he was a bit of a bore about his craze of the moment, which was playing the guitar.

We left the castle by the north gates and made for Vannich Village, which is on the coast of the Firth, and, having passed through the village, we turned inland again and drove in among the hills.

'Strathdonan is only about sixteen miles from the castle as the crow flies,' Aunt told Mr. Cameron, 'but Ben Vannich comes in between and we have to go round about it.'

'We sure can't go over the top of it,' Mr. Cameron said, looking up at the high peak where, on the north side, there was still a streak of snow.

'It is a pimple compared with your Canadian Rockies,' Aunt said.

'On the face of a little country like Scotland, that is no pimple.'

'Actually, it is quite a treacherous hill,' Aunt agreed.

Inland, we drove for a time along the bank of the River Vannich and then forked on to a roughish road over a flat moor, but soon we began to climb a bit and on the brow of a hill where the road went over and down into a glen, Aunt pointed ahead: 'This glen below us is Strathdonan. That is the house, down at the bottom, among the trees.'

We could not see any house, only this clump of trees and they were all conifers, so that, from this distance, they looked

D

black. The farther we went down into this glen, the farther
away the sun and the sky seemed to get, and the hills seemed
to close right in, dimming the colour of the grass down
below, and, when the road took a turn, a small loch came
into sight, but it was overhung by the dark-brown hills and
its water was dull black and still, without a sparkle on it
anywhere. Even in the big car, with the chauffeur on one
side and Fifth on the other and Aunt and Mr. Cameron
behind, I had a creepy feeling of being all alone in a world
suddenly gone silent and Aunt's voice sounded queer and
strained when she said: 'It always seems to be dark in
Strathdonan.'

'A cloud just passed over the sun there,' Mr. Cameron
said in his creaky practical voice. 'You always get cloud in
hill country. The young fellah bought this place lock, stock
and barrel, you said? Interesting to see what he's gotten for
his money. That fellah is nobody's fool.'

'I shouldn't think there is much lock, stock or barrel left.
The last Gordon got to the bottom of everything,' Aunt said,
'but the land alone is worth what Somerled paid for the
whole place. No other local person would touch Strathdonan,
you know, and Somerled's first offer was accepted.'

'Wouldn't touch it out of superstition, you mean? Never
heard such hooey in my life!' Mr. Cameron said angrily as
the cars stopped, one behind the other, at a big front door
of unpainted greyish wood that frowned down from the
top of five wide stone steps.

It was a horrid-looking house. It was built of grey stone
which was nearly covered with black-looking ivy and it had
three storeys of windows that looked like dull eyes, staring
down at us with hatred. Added on to one end of this square
block there was a long L-shaped wing of only two storeys,

this also draped in black ivy and with the same hating windows staring down. The dark trees — spruces and firs — crowded round the house close to the walls, some of the spruces as tall as the house itself, with the pointed dark fingers of their branches touching the walls and the roof and, under these trees, there was no grass, only a thick, dark carpet of fallen needles that led away into gloomy caverns of underbrush.

Somerled got out of the car with a big old key in his hand, put it in the lock of the door and at last got it to turn with a horrid creak, whereupon he put his shoulder against the wood and the door groaned open as if it were unwilling to open at all. 'Welcome to Strathdonan, everybody,' he said and I noticed that even his bright red-gold hair looked dull and colourless as if the gaping blackness of the hall inside the door were reaching out and covering it like a thunder-cloud covering the top of Ben Vannich.

We were all standing at the foot of the steps, but I felt that I could not move and Aunt, too, seemed to feel like this, although Somerled and everybody were waiting for her to go in, and, at last, old Mr. Cameron became impatient and went creaking and stumping up the steps and into the hall. Then we all followed, Aunt and I coming last and I feeling that I wanted to stick very close to her and even hold on to her hand.

'Don't you like it, Shona?' Somerled asked, smiling down at me as I passed him in the doorway.

'It's awfully sort of dark,' I said feebly because I did not like to tell him that I simply loathed this new possession of his because I love all Somerled's other things like his aunts and the castle and the blue family banner with the White Hind of Vannich on it.

'We'll soon pull the blinds up,' he said and now he went ahead of us all into a room on the left, where he opened heavy wooden shutters and pulled up a black blind from the window.

We found ourselves in a largish square room with dirty paper on the walls, a dusty threadbare carpet and some neglected-looking furniture, but there was a pretty fireplace with a mantel which had little embossed garlands on it, and there were more garlands making a pattern on the plastered ceiling.

'What's the matter with this?' old Mr. Cameron said to Aunt in his angry-sounding way and giving one wall a thump with his stick. 'Good sound building. No sign of worm or dry rot or anything!'

'This older part is charming,' Aunt agreed. 'The new part is not so fine, though.'

'Good sound building this,' the old man said and went creaking out into the hall.

We went all over this older part, which was the main block of the house and, although it was all filthy and terribly neglected, you could see that it could be made into a charming place. When we came downstairs again, Somerled opened a door under the staircase and we felt a dank draught of cold air as he shone his torch down some stone steps.

'Cellars,' he said. 'Wonder what's down there?'

He went down a little way, waving the torch about until its beam fell on a great heap of empty bottles. There must have been — not exaggerating — about a thousand of them and Somerled said to Aunt: 'No ghosts or skeletons, Liz. Only Gordon's empty whisky bottles,' and everybody laughed, but neither Aunt nor Angus laughed: they merely looked round at us all in a wait-and-see sort of way until Angus said: 'Him That Used To Live Here lived in an upside-down sort of way. Most gentlemen keep the wine in the cellar and bring it up to empty the bottle, but *he* emptied the bottle and then threw it down into the cellar.'

When Mr. Gordon had been alive, Angus used to jerk his head in the direction of this house and call him 'Him Over There,' never calling him by his proper name, which is Angus's way of being most insulting about anyone, for Angus is meticulous about giving people their proper names and titles, always calling Miss Dotty and Miss Coocoo 'Miss Dorothy and Miss Constance' and never calling Somerled anything except 'Macdonald' and always referring to him as 'the Macdonald,' which is his title as Chieftain of the Vannich Macdonalds.

Somerled now opened a door that led from the hall into the L-shaped wing and Aunt said to Mr. Cameron: 'This wing was added by the Gordon who won the estate from Somerled the Gambler. Gordon married a high-born English wife and tried to turn Strathdonan into an English mansion but not with much success, in my opinion. He hadn't enough money to do it properly.'

While we had been going over the old part of the house, I had quite forgotten the creepy feeling I had had when we first saw it from outside, but as soon as we were in the large, musty, drawing-room in this new wing the air seemed to become very chill as if a damp mist were coming down and the creepy feeling came back. I went close to Aunt and was comforted when she laid her hand on my shoulder and kept it there while we looked about this room when Somerled had opened the shutters. It was very large and had once been prettily furnished, but the silk curtains had faded and rotted and hung in long tatters and everything smelled of staleness and damp, as if neither doors nor windows had been opened for years.

Old Mr. Cameron was poking about with his stick and his fingers, like a wise old tortoise looking for a dry comfortable bed for the winter. He at last turned up a corner of the rotten carpet, which fell to powder as he moved it, and said: 'This isn't so good, young fellah. Damp. Rotten. All the wood-work's shot to hell. Look at that!' And he thumped the floorboards with the point of his stick so that it went right through and a stronger smell of damp seemed to ooze up through the hole. 'The walls are all right, but you'll have to gut the wood out and start from scratch.'

'It's all right as long as the walls and roof are sound,' Somerled said.

It took a long time to go through all the rooms with Mr. Cameron poking and prodding about, so that Fifth and Neil and Donald became bored and went off to explore the up-stairs part of this wing without waiting for the rest of us. I would have gone with them had it not been for the creepy coldness of the place which neither Fifth nor my brothers seemed to have noticed, but I preferred to stay with Aunt.

It is difficult to describe the eerie uneasiness of that place. Sometimes it was so real that it made me shiver, and some-times it was not there at all, so that I wondered if it was all imagination and brought on by the things that Aunt and Angus had said about this house. Father is always rather stern in a kind sort of way with Neil, Donald and me if we lose our heads when anything dangerous happens, like the time I forgot about our old electric iron which has no thermo-stat until it had burned right through the ironing-board Panic is infectious, Father says, and that is why we should try to keep calm, and I wondered if Aunt's and Angus's spooky feelings were infectious too and if I were simply catching this eerie uneasiness from them. Anyhow, the three of us kept close together while Mr. Cameron and Somerled poked about, being very practical and not in the least spooky.

When we went upstairs, Mr. Cameron was better pleased. It was not so damp up here and the woodwork was in quite good condition and so was the roof, so that he became quite cock-a-hoop and said that Somerled had made a very good buy. We were standing in a long sort of corridor with windows at intervals along one wall, and Aunt said: 'This was Gordon's idea of a Long Gallery, but it is a long way behind Chatsworth, I am afraid.'

It was very dreary with faded walls and less-faded green patches where a lot of pictures had been removed, leaving only one of a very sad-looking stag standing on top of a hill peering into the mist or it may only have been dirt on the canvas. Off this corridor, a lot of doors opened into small rooms, some of which had beds in them, some of which were empty, and Somerled and Mr. Cameron agreed that here they had, ready-made, twenty bedrooms for skiers and became more pleased than ever with themselves.

I was standing looking at the stag in the picture and feeling sorry for it in this dreary place all by itself, when the three boys came dashing out of a room at the far end and ran helter-skelter past us.

'There's a monkey in the trees outside!' said Neil and he and Fifth rushed on and down the stairs, but Aunt, with the hand that was not on my shoulder, reached out, grabbed Donald and said: 'A monkey?' 'Yes,' said Donald, wriggling free, 'we saw its shadow on the wall!' and he dashed off after the others.

Somerled and Mr. Cameron merely smiled and went on

poking into the next room, but Aunt and Angus looked at one another over the top of my head.

'A shadow on the wall?' Aunt whispered.

'Now, now Elizabeth,' Angus said very quietly, 'we will just go downstairs and outside. Come, now.'

'No, Angus. I mustn't be an idiot. I am going along there,' and, taking her hand from my shoulder, she marched away along the corridor towards the doorway where the boys had rushed out. Angus took my hand in his and we followed her, but when we went into the room there was not a thing except Aunt standing in the middle of the floor. It had dirty paper on the walls, dust on the floor and cobwebs everywhere, but it was lighter than the other rooms, for it was the end one of the wing and had windows on two sides, from one of which I could see the cars down below, while the other looked towards the dark loch with a broken stone jetty on the shore. Even with two windows, the light was still dimmish because of the great trees outside so close to the windows, and I found myself wishing that I had eyes on all four sides of me so that I could look at all four walls at once. But it was obvious when I looked round at the walls that there could be no shadow of anything—the light was too dim to make shadows.

'The sun must have blinked out for a moment and have made the trees cast a shadow,' Aunt said, which made us look out at the branches of the tall spruces, which might indeed have been black grotesque arms or wings, rather, like the webbed wings of gigantic bats. She smiled at Angus and me in a shaky sort of way. 'Still, let's go outside now, shall we? I don't really believe in the—the *thing*, but I still don't like this house.'

'Neither do I,' I said.

'Nor I,' said Angus. 'There is an evil feel about the place and it is more than woodworm or dampness.' We left the room, went along the corridor, down the stairs and out into the open, and only then did I feel that it was possible to breathe properly again.

It was cold and dull outside among all those black trees, and the three of us got into Somerled's car. When the door was shut and I felt safe, I looked out at the ivy-covered walls of the house and said: 'Aunt, I wonder what the boys really saw?'

'I have behaved very badly, Shona,' she said, 'and your father would be furious with me, but there have been all sorts of stories of queer things being seen here for the past hundred and fifty years, although I have never heard of a monkey being seen before.' She laughed a little. 'The stories are probably a lot of nonsense, but I got a fright when the boys rushed past. There are usually reasonable explanations for all the queer things like the Ghost Piper of Castle Vannich being merely the wind in a certain direction.'

'I can't think of a reasonable explanation of why that drawing-room *feels* so horrid,' I said, looking out at the windows of that room. Aunt and Angus also looked out. 'And the Gordons have been such tragic people,' Aunt said. 'It is as if this house hated them ever since they came to it. Not one of the Gordon owners died a natural death when you think of it, Angus.'

'That is true,' Angus agreed as Somerled and Mr. Cameron at last came out and Somerled locked the door. 'But maybe,' Angus went on, 'things will take a turn for the better now that it is back in Macdonald hands.'

'I hope so, Angus,' Aunt said as we got out of the car.

'There's a good bit of money in the trees alone,' Mr.

Cameron was saying, 'and the first thing you do is to get them felled right away and get that creeper torn off the stonework. You got a fine place here, young fellah, if you go about it the right way and listen to what I tell you. Now, where is this glen in my great-grandfather's bible?'

'We can't go there today,' Aunt said. 'There is no motor road and, besides, we have to get back.'

Mr. Cameron raised his stick, ready to shake it at her, but she went on: 'Somerled will lend us his Land-Rover to drive to the Broad Glen, I am sure, but another day.' She glanced at the house behind her. 'Sufficient unto the day is the evil thereof. Where are those boys?'

The boys appeared out of the dark caverns beneath the trees. 'No monkey, Grandpa,' said Fifth, shaking his head, 'couldn't have been a monkey up here anyways, but the shadow certainly looked like a monkey.'

'Monkey yourself,' said Mr. Cameron angrily. 'Get in the car.' He turned to Somerled. 'I can borrow this Land-Rover of yours tomorrow?'

'Certainly, sir. Any time.'

'Good.' He now turned to Aunt and me. 'We'll go to my great-grandfather's glen tomorrow, huh?'

'Oh, all right,' Aunt said, 'but I've never seen such a hustler. If you are going to live in the Highlands, you must learn a slower pace, Mr. Cameron.'

'I been a hustler all my life and can't stop now,' he said. 'All right. Let's get back to the castle. What we waiting for?' He waved the stick at us, chasing us all into the cars, and we drove up and out of the dark glen of Strathdonan into the sunshine of the open moor.

4. The Ghost of a Graveyard

THE next morning, the fourth Mr. Cameron got into the driving seat of the Land-Rover; Aunt sat in the middle seat, Fifth and I climbed into the back; and we all set off for the ruined church in the broad part of Glen Vannich.

When we set off, nobody except old Mr. Cameron was in a very good temper. He was pleased because he was getting all his own way, and the rest of us were displeased because we were not getting any of *our* way. Aunt said there were a dozen and one things that she ought to be doing that morning, and Fifth and his father were annoyed because they had wanted to go to Strathdonan with Somerled, who was taking a gang of men there to start felling the trees round the house. And I was annoyed at having to go just to please old Mr.

Cameron, when my going made Somerled so angry. I could not think why, but when, after breakfast, he heard I was going, he was simply furious.

'There is no reason for Shona to be entirely at the beck and call of that comic dynasty of Camerons,' he said to Aunt. 'That old man hasn't bought us all.'

Only the day before, he and Mr. Cameron had been the best of friends and Aunt looked as puzzled as I felt when she said: 'Somerled, don't *you* get cranky next. I can't bear it. After he has done this trip you must take him to Strathdonan and keep him amused over there.'

'Say, are we going to this glen today or next year?' old Mr. Cameron bellowed from the doorway, and we all went scuttling out and jumped into the Land-Rover while Somerled watched us with that thundery look on his face, so Fifth and I waved to cheer him up, but it seemed only to make him angrier than ever.

We drove to Vannich Village again, but, today, instead of forking to the left and over the moor after we left the riverside, Mr. Fourth drove to the right over rough grassland where sheep were grazing all around. This part of Glen Vannich, near the coast, is a broadish plain, actually, with the river winding through it, and over on our right we could see the little wooden bridge called Half Sovereign Bridge which leads across the river to the track that goes up to Angus's house under the Ben.

Following the sheep track across the flat glen, we soon came to the clump of trees which grows round the ruins of the church. There are a broken belfry, a few bits of broken wall, and that is all.

'Well, there it is, Mr. Cameron,' Aunt said. 'That is all that remains of the crofter township of Glen Vannich.'

We looked at the ruin, then turned our backs to it and looked out over the wide plain of green grass where the sheep grazed and the lambs played in the sunshine while Ben Vannich, away on the other side beyond the river, looked half-asleep in the bright light, as if it were thinking of old, old secrets. It was difficult to believe that once this green valley had been dotted with little houses, with fields about them where men worked while the women hung out washing and the children laughed and shouted as they played all around.

Old Mr. Cameron sighed and then said: 'You told me you had located the site of the graveyard. How? This looks like a clean sweep to me.'

Aunt sat down on one of the fallen stones of the church and opened her handbag, and we all sat down around her. Out of the bag she took a square black-and-white photograph, a picture taken from the air, such as you sometimes see in the newspapers.

'During the war,' she said, 'I worked in the Photographic Branch of Intelligence and I found out that things can be seen on aerial photographs which are not visible in any other way. Last year, when I began work on the Vannich history, it suddenly occurred to me that an aerial picture might tell us something, so I wrote to an old colleague who now works with a civil firm of aerial surveyors and he sent me this. It is only a chance shot, taken when they were surveying for the new dam, and it doesn't show much, but it is something. You see that whitish line there, there, very faintly there and here?' She pointed on the picture with a pin taken from her hair, forming a little rectangle. 'There has been a wall there at some time. The earth has been disturbed, rubble has got mixed with it and the nature of the grass is a little different. By refraction of light and a lot of things you would understand better than I do, the aerial camera picks up these tiny differences.'

'We use aerial survey a lot in the firm,' Mr. Fourth said, 'but not in this way. Very interesting.'

'Archaeologists are using it more and more,' Aunt told him. 'You see these?' She pointed to several little grey dots. 'These are very probably the sites of some of the croft houses.' There was something ghostly about the faint grey outline of the graveyard and the little dots where the houses had been.

'Listen, where's this friend of yours that gave you this picture?' old Mr. Cameron asked.

'Glasgow. Why?'

'We'll get him up here to take some decent pictures. That thing is the darndest bit of aerial survey I ever saw!'

'It was only a chance shot!' Aunt protested. 'I was glad to get it!'

Old Mr. Cameron ignored her. 'Son,' he said to Mr. Fourth, 'when we get back, you get on the phone to this guy and tell him I want a decent coverage of this area as soon as he can get a plane up here.' He grabbed the photograph, peered at it angrily in his short-sighted way and then handed it back to Aunt: 'Where's the church here on it?'

'There.'

'So'—he looked at the picture and then round about—'the graveyard was that way? The other side of the track?'

'Yes.' Aunt got up. 'Come, Shona. Come, Fifth and you too, Mr. Fourth.'

On the other side of the track she began to take long strides, counting as she went along, and then she said: 'You stand here, Shona.' Then she went striding on at right angles over the grass until she had placed Mr. Fourth and Fifth in certain positions and last of all herself. Then she called: 'These are approximately the four corners, Mr. Cameron.'

We then went back to where he was sitting and he said: 'Darn it! I'll rebuild that wall if it's the last thing I do. Got any good stonemasons around here?'

'Plenty of them,' Aunt told him.

'Son,' he commanded, 'you see to it. Get some good pictures from this guy in Glasgow, get the site properly established and get some builders. We'll put a wall round the graveyard with a gate facing the church here. And we'll get this ruin shored up so it don't fall any further but we'll leave it looking like a ruin as a monument to that Gordon bunch. Well, get moving. There's no time to waste. I want to see that wall up before I go back to Toronto.' He jerked off towards the Land-Rover and Aunt scuttled after him to get into her place in the middle, but just then a boy of about Neil's age suddenly dropped from a low branch of a tree beside the church and stood looking at us.

'Hello, Findlay,' Aunt said, stopping and smiling at him. 'What are you doing away up here?'

He did not speak, but merely stood there looking uncertain, and he made me think of my little brother Iain when visitors he has never seen before come to our house. Iain is mentally-handicapped, as it is called, but he is everybody's favourite person in our family and I knew that this boy, although older, was another like Iain. Aunt went towards him and he smiled at her while still darting half-afraid little glances at the rest of us, and when she was quite close to him, he pointed as if he felt secure now and said: 'Girl.'

'Yes, Findlay,' Aunt said, 'that is Shona.'

'Shona,' he repeated carefully and then pointed at Fifth. 'Boy.'

'Yes, that is Evan.'

'Evan.' He pointed at old Mr. Cameron. 'Old 'an,' he said and then he saw Mr. Fourth on the other side of the Land-Rover and shrank back, looking frightened and pointing: '*Bad* 'an!' he said.

'Oh, no, Findlay. No bad men here,' Aunt told him. 'Would you like to come for a ride in the car with Shona and Evan?'

'No!' he said sharply, drawing back towards the wall and still pointing at Mr. Fourth. 'Bad 'an!'

'No, Findlay,' Aunt said again. 'No bad men here,' but the boy suddenly ran away and climbed up one of the tall trees as swiftly as a monkey and, feeling safe up there it seemed, he waved to us gaily and called: ''bye!'

Aunt asked Mr. Fourth to stop at a cottage in Vannich Village which was Findlay's home, and a pretty, white-haired lady came down the path to the gate.

'Findlay is away up the Glen at the old church, Mrs. Elton,' Aunt said, 'climbing trees.'

The old lady smiled. 'Findlay is always roaming about the glen and the shore and he is always climbing too nowadays, Miss Cameron, but he will come home when he is hungry,' she said.

She came close to the car and looked gravely past old Mr. Cameron and into Aunt's face. 'Could you spare the time to come to see me any day? There is something I would like you to advise me about if you will be so kind.'

'I'll come as soon as I can, Mrs. Elton. I am glad to see Findlay so much better. I would have been to see you before, but I have been busy.'

E

'I know how busy you are, and I am very grateful that you can come at all. And this is your niece?' she asked, looking at me. 'When your aunt comes to see me, perhaps you and your brothers will come and visit Findlay?'

'Yes, we shall all come, Mrs. Elton,' Aunt promised.

We got back to the castle in time for lunch and when we got out of the Land-Rover Somerled, who was sitting on the Stirrup Stone with Angus, glowered and said to Aunt and me: 'I must say you took a goodish time to look at a ruin. I thought you must be rebuilding the old church.'

'We practically were,' Aunt told him.

'Yes,' I said. 'Somerled, Mr. Cameron is going to have the graveyard wall rebuilt. Isn't it splendid?'

'What?' he said, glowering even more.

When Aunt had explained Mr. Cameron's plan, he looked angrier than ever, gave me a sulky glare and said: 'So you think this is all splendid?'

'Well, it is rather, isn't it?' I said feebly.

'You've got a disease called dollar-dazzle,' he told me and strode away into the house.

I felt hurt and sort of limp. I had never known Somerled to be like this before and it seemed to be the Camerons from Canada who had this effect on him.

'Aunt,' I said when we were washing our hands, 'what is the matter with Somerled?'

She smiled. 'Take no notice of him, Shona. His red-haired nose is a little out of joint, that's all. He has come to regard us Camerons as his own special property rather, and he is annoyed because we are giving a little attention to the Camerons from Canada.'

'But I thought he would be pleased about the rebuilding of the wall and everything. He is always saying he wished he had more money to spend on the old features of the estate.'

'He will be pleased in the end. But old Mr. Cameron's way of doing things to other people's property is a little high-handed. Somerled himself is high-handed, too, so it is a case of Greek meeting Greek, but old Mr. Cameron is better equipped with money — good sound Canadian dollars.'

'But it isn't only old Mr. Cameron. Somerled called Fifth a pimply little twerp this morning and Fifth has no dollars much and has never been high-handed. He hasn't got pimples either,' I added.

Aunt smiled again. 'Don't take the slightest notice of anything Somerled says, Shona. And don't let him make you angry or unhappy or, at least, don't let him see you looking angry or hurt. Simply ignore him and he will come to his senses. He is a bit of a spoilt darling and in his own way he is just as cranky as old Mr. Cameron.'

It was easy for Aunt to tell me to ignore Somerled, but it is not so easy to ignore somebody who is over six feet, clumping about in heavy brogues and a kilt, being nasty and sarcastic every time you cross his path, with his hair getting redder and redder, so I began to avoid Somerled altogether and went about with my brothers and Fifth when I was not with Aunt or old Mr. Cameron or helping Miss Dotty and Miss Coocoo to cut hexagonals of tartan. In a place the size of Castle Vannich, it was easy to keep out of Somerled's way and, besides, he was away at Strathdonan for part of every day now that the work had begun.

By the end of about a week, Aunt and I had less of old Mr. Cameron, too, because the aerial photographs came, the real situation of the graveyard was established, and men

were already cutting the turf so that the foundations of the
new wall could be laid as soon as some masons could be
hustled out from Rioch. Mr. Cameron with his son drove
away every day to the old church and sometimes Fifth, my
brothers and I went with them, but not if there was anything
more exciting to do.

One morning, though, I met Somerled on the narrow
corkscrew stairs down from our floor and there we were,
face to face, between the rough old stone walls, Somerled
looking bigger and angrier than ever in this narrow place.

'I suppose you are going graveyarding with that lot
again?' he said.

'If you mean the Camerons from Canada,' I said, 'I'm
not.'

I felt that I was being rude to my host at Castle Vannich,
but I did not care. And I was not ignoring him as Aunt had
told me to do, but I did not care about that either. If he can
be rude and angry, I thought, I can be rude and angry too,
but, suddenly, he was not rude or angry any more and,
instead, smiled down at me in his old way and said: 'Shona,
come to Strathdonan. It isn't dark any more. You'll like it
now.'

He made it sound as if he were having all those hideous
trees at Strathdonan cut down simply to please me, but I
knew that this was not so. They were being cut because
they were too close to the house and dangerous to the walls
and the roof.

'I know enough about them to beware of their red-haired
charm,' I seemed to hear the echo of Aunt's voice saying.

'No, thank you,' I said to Somerled.

'But Shona, why not?' He sounded quite hurt. 'I'd like
you to see it now.'

'Another time perhaps,' I said. 'I have something else to do today.'

'What?' he snapped at me.

Actually, I was going with Aunt and the boys to visit Mrs. Elton and Findlay that afternoon and could easily have told him so, but I was remembering how horrible he had been and I remembered what Father says when we ask questions about things that are none of our business.

'Is that relevant in the circumstances?' I asked and then slipped through between him and the wall and ran all the way down to Aunt's office.

It was pleasant at Mrs. Elton's house, much pleasanter than at the castle, for there was nobody there who got into tantrums for no obvious reason. Mrs. Elton was a sweet old lady, with smiling blue eyes and pretty white hair and she sat sewing at a tartan cushion while she talked to Aunt. Neil, Donald and I went down to the shore of the Firth with Findlay. We spent a sunny happy afternoon, but, coming back in the car, Aunt was very quiet and thoughtful and even a little worried, I thought, and she continued like this until late evening, when she asked me to get the boys off to bed.

It may seem odd that somebody has to get a boy of fourteen and a boy of nine off to bed, but if you have somebody in the family like our nine-year-old Donald nothing is odd. Donald cannot keep his mind on things like brushing his teeth or taking his clothes off — this mind of his is always too busy with more interesting things. Once, when he put himself to bed, he was found in the morning to have slept in his pyjama top and his football boots, which he had forgotten to take off. Neil, who shares a room with him, is absolutely useless because he undresses himself, washes and cleans his teeth in his own efficient and automatic way while he listens all the time to Donald telling him the weight of a whale's liver or about the Spanish Inquisition or whatever is the latest thing that Donald has been reading about. Neil is much too interested, always, in listening to what Donald is saying to notice the clothes that he is not taking off or the teeth he is not brushing.

So, when I went up to their room on this evening, there was Neil, lying in bed, all clean and smelling of toothpaste while Donald was sitting fully dressed and very grubby in the middle of the floor. He had taken off one shoe and was scratching his head with the muddy toe of it while he stared at the sky beyond the window.

'Donald,' I said, 'get up and into the bathroom at once.'

He looked in my direction, but I do not think he saw me. 'It was in the newspaper,' he said, still scratching his head with the shoe, 'shortly after Christmas.'

When Donald is like this, Mother says it drives her up the wall and now I knew exactly what she meant. If we had been at home, I would have done what Mother does, which is to run downstairs and say to Father: 'Go up and see if you can do anything with that boy. He is completely Cameron tonight.'

And then Father laughs and says: 'But come now, *you* are his mother,' and Mother, not laughing at all, says: 'John, don't argue. In *my* family, we have nobody like Liz, after all.' Mother always quotes Aunt as the reason why Donald is as he is, which makes no sense, but seems to make Mother feel better. But Father was not here and I felt no better, so I shook Donald's shoulder and said: 'Donald, wake up and get undressed.'

'Shooting tragedy at Strathdonan,' he said, staring at the wall as if he were reading a headline that was printed there. 'Death strikes again in the shadowed glen.'

I now sat down on the floor, too, and Neil sat up in his bed.

'Donald,' I said, 'what are you talking about?'

'It was in the newspaper,' he repeated and began to put on the shoe he had taken off, so I took it away from him and began to unlace the other one. This is how it is with Donald. We all try not to do things for him and make him do them for himself, but he always wins by what Father calls 'the sullen power of sheer inertia!'

'Go on, Muggins!' said Neil from the bed. 'What else did the newspaper say?'

'And that photograph of Aunt wearing her hat,' said Donald dreamily. So now I suppose I have to tell about Aunt's hat. Aunt owns only one hat because she never wears hats. Father and Mother were married in Aberdeen and Aunt arrived an hour before the wedding without a hat, so that was when the hat got bought. Aunt is not a good subject for hats, and this hat was bought in a hurry. It is not a success. There is only one photograph of Aunt, too, because she says she is not glamorous enough to be photographed and not interesting enough to be painted, but a pressman got a photograph of her at the wedding and, being the only one, it gets into the newspapers now and again. And, of course, she is wearing the hat. As I have said, I was nearly sixteen at this time and I had been haunted by this hat all my life. Hats get a little out of date in over sixteen years even if they are successful at the time they are bought, and this hat, I repeat, was never a success.

'What had Aunt in her hat got to do with this that you were saying about Strathdonan?' I asked Donald.

'It is true that Strathdonan has for long been a tragic house, commented Elizabeth Cameron, noted Highland writer, in an exclusive interview with this paper,' Donald said, as if he were reading the words off the wall again.

'But what *happened*?' Neil asked angrily. 'What was the shooting tragedy?'

Donald suddenly became practical, stood up and undressed himself completely in about two seconds, leaving his clothes in a heap on the floor.

'There was this man Gordon,' he said, 'shot his wife and then shot himself and left a note saying he had done it.' He became dreamy and stared at the wall again. 'Murder and suicide while the balance of the mind was disturbed, the court decreed,' he said in his remembering quoting voice, 'but historically, this was the tragic end of a tragic story.' He changed to his practical voice again: 'Shona, I don't have to wash, do I? I'm quite clean.'

'Bathroom,' I said, pointing across the passage and followed him to see that he at least scraped the mud off his neck.

It was late before Aunt came upstairs and both the boys were asleep but I was still reading when she came into my room.

'I thought you would be asleep,' she said, yawning.

'No. I wanted to ask you about a thing Donald was telling about Strathdonan. He says that he read in the newspaper that Mr. Gordon shot his wife and then shot himself. Just after Christmas, Donald said it was. Aunt, is it true?'

'Yes. I am afraid so.'

'How horrible!'

'Yes.'

'Was Mr. Gordon mad?'

'I think that people are always mad in the moment that they commit murder,' Aunt said. 'But Mr. Gordon drank heavily and he and his wife lived in a very queer way. They came to Strathdonan a few years ago and, of course, we all called on them—people like Dotty and Coocoo and myself —the way we do in country districts like this, to make them feel welcome, you know. We were all delighted that Strathdonan had been opened up after lying empty for years. But they did not want us to call on them or welcome them. They didn't want anybody. I stayed for only about five minutes and they hardly spoke to me, but simply sat, waiting for me to go away.' She shivered. 'It was in that tattered old drawing-room. It was horrible. And this is how they behaved to everybody, so none of us went again. And then, they never came out. They had an arrangement with the grocer, who left a box of things on the doorstep, but he never saw them. They lived like hermits.'

'How very queer,' I said, feeling shivery too as I thought of that dark house among the trees.

'As Angus says, there is nothing queerer than people,' Aunt said, preparing to go.

'Angus always said that Mr. Gordon was a poacher,' I said.

'He prowled about at night a lot and he always had a gun over his arm, but I don't think he bothered with poaching. I used to see him through my field-glasses when I was reporting the flights of the wild geese for the Ornithological Society two years ago. He was always going home just about dawn, like an owl or some creature that lives by night. You must go to sleep now, Shona, and not worry your head over the Gordons. They are dead now and perhaps it is just as well. I think they must have been very unhappy.'

'If I had been his wife,' I said, 'I wouldn't have stayed all alone in that horrible house at night while he prowled about outside.'

'What his wife felt is something that we shall never know, but she stayed with him. There can be queer bonds between people, Shona. People can love people who make them very unhappy. In spite of all the unhappiness, they go on loving and have to stay, rather like Mr. Gordon being a drunkard. All drunkards really hate the alcohol that stupefies them and makes them mad, but they go on drinking it all the same.'

'I don't understand.'

'It is very difficult to understand, but you have to accept it as true. And now you really must go to sleep. Mrs. Elton is a charming person, isn't she?'

' Yes, and Findlay is a darling.'

' I'd like you and Neil and Donald to see a bit more of Findlay. He is lonely. The village children are a little scared of him and of course he is scared of strangers too.'

' Mrs. Elton is English, isn't she? ' I asked.

' No. She has an English accent because she left the Highlands when she was fifteen to go to domestic service in London. Her husband was English, but Mrs. Elton was born in Ross-shire here.'

' And where are Findlay's parents? '

' Findlay is an orphan. That is why he lives with his grandmother.'

' Poor Findlay! Good-night, Aunt.'

Before I went to sleep, I thought that Neil, Donald, Iain and I were very lucky people with Father and Mother, Grandpa and Grandma, who are Mother's parents, and Aunt and all the other people we have. I had never before thought much about being fortunate in this way, and it was very comforting to think of it now, especially when I remembered Iain, for people like Iain and Findlay have even more need than the rest of us to have people of their own around them to protect them and love them. I decided that, in the morning, I would get Neil and Donald to ask Somerled to drop us at Findlay's home on his way to Strathdonan. He was quite his usual self with Neil and Donald because they were less involved than I was with the Camerons from Canada.

5. An Invisible Mischief-maker

OLD Mr. Cameron became much too interested in the rebuilding of the graveyard wall and the work that was going on at Strathdonan to want to have me tagging along as his personal attendant, and things became much more normal. Some days, my brothers and I went to call on Findlay and his grandmother, some days we went on the loch fishing with one of the ghillies, and some days I spent with Aunt in her office or helping out in the tea-room.

Somerled continued to be touchy and bad-tempered sometimes, but he went over to Strathdonan most days and I did not see him very much and hardly ever to speak to until one evening, shortly before dinner, when I was in her office with Aunt, he came in, looking very worried.

'There is something very queer going on at Strathdonan,' he blurted out to Aunt as if he hated to admit that anything queer could happen there.

'Oh?' she said. 'Such as?'

'We had a load of planks delivered. They were stacked in the drive under a tarpaulin last night. This morning half of them were floating in the middle of the loch.'

'Who in the world would do a thing like that?' Aunt asked, and Somerled looked relieved.

'I thought you might suggest it was the work of the ghost,' he said.

'No. I don't believe in that sort of ghost. Has anything else happened?'

'Quite a lot. Windows broken, a gallon can of paint emptied out on to the gravel, and one of the carpenters' tool-kits has disappeared. It is beginning to upset the men rather badly.'

'You must get on to the police, Somerled, and put a watchman on the place at night.'

'A watchman? I'd have to do it myself. Nobody else would stay there at night. Would you?'

'Oh, yes. I'd stand watch for a human vandal and nuisance, for that is all this is.'

'I don't understand you,' Somerled said, 'or Angus either. He said just what you have said and yet you two were the ones who told me to have nothing to do with the place. I thought you would be bound to believe, as the men do, that these things are supernatural.'

'Don't be silly,' said Aunt.

'But nothing like this has happened in the district before! I called at the police station in the village on my way home and the sergeant said he has had no reports of any mischief of this kind for over two years. In fact, when I told him about it, he looked pop-eyed and began to go on about Strath-donan being an uncanny place.'

'Rubbish!' Aunt said. 'Strathdonan is uncanny all right, but to throw planks into a loch and steal carpenters' tools is not uncanny — these things are pure malicious mischief. Your trouble is some *body*, Somerled, not some thing, and if it goes on you will have to put a watchman on the place.' Her eyes gleamed. Aunt can be very mischievous sometimes, I had discovered just these holidays.

'Why don't you and the Camerons from Canada set up house over there? It would save you miles of travelling every day.' But if Aunt and I expected Somerled to get as furious as usual about the Camerons, we were disappointed, for he said: 'By gosh, that's a jolly good idea! To lie in wait and catch this thief would be exactly that old boy's cup of tea, I should think, and I am sure the grandson fancies himself as a sleuth.'

Somerled went away and Aunt looked at me and made a comic face.

'What do you bet a pantechnicon will leave here tomorrow for Strathdonan, carrying beds for Somerled, the Camerons and the secretaries?' she asked.

And that was more or less what happened — not the next day, exactly, but by the end of the week old Mr. Cameron, Mr. Fourth, Fifth, the secretaries and one chauffeur, Somerled and Angus had moved over to Strathdonan, leaving Mrs. Cameron and one chauffeur at Castle Vannich.

Sometimes, people seem to be very contrary. Aunt began to talk a lot about Strathdonan, wondering how the work was going on, wondering how it looked now that most of the trees had been cut down, and Miss Dotty and Miss Coo-coo, who had said that they would never set foot in Strathdonan even if you paid them, began to get bored with their tartan cushions and fancied a drive over to Strathdonan.

Perhaps contrariness, like panic and spookiness, is infectious, for I, too, began to feel that I would like to see Strathdonan and that all the creepiness that I had felt when I was there was simply a lot of nonsense and, besides, Castle Vannich was not the same with Somerled and Angus never there at all.

So, one Friday, Aunt and I drove off to Strathdonan. Neil and Donald had been there lots of times since that first visit and chose to go fishing on the loch instead. Miss Dotty and Miss Coocoo got into their own car to follow Aunt and me, but they stopped in the village to give some tartan patches to one of the cushion-makers, forgot where they were really going and did not arrive at Strathdonan at all.

When Aunt drove over the brow of the hill into the glen where the house lay, I could hardly believe that we had come to the right place, it all looked so different. All the trees in front of the house had been cut down so that you could see the building on the other side of the loch and also see it reflected in the water. Aunt stopped the car and we both sat, looking.

'It is a very dignified house, seen from here,' she said. 'When all that mess of earth and branches between it and the loch is turned into green grass, it will be rather beautiful.'

She got out of the car and stood looking around her, so I got out too. The pass where the rough road came over into the glen was a little like a chip in the edge of a saucer and Aunt's car was sitting in the V of the chip, as it were, with a slope rising to the left and a much higher hill going up on the right. It was at this higher hill that Aunt was looking.

'I wonder,' she said, aloud but to herself, speaking in a way that Donald often does.

'What, Aunt?'

She leaned against the car and looked up at the grassy

slope of the hill, her eyes looking far away, as if she had not heard me speak.

'It was on the other side of that hill that the aeroplane crashed, remember?' I asked, to remind her that I was there and to bring her back from what Father calls her Celtic Twilight.

'I remember,' she said dreamily, not thinking about the aeroplane crash. 'I wonder.'

'Wonder *what*, Aunt?'

'Sorry.' She stopped looking at the hill and looked at me now, not dreaming any more. 'There was what seems to have been a very fine carved Celtic stone in this glen once,' she said, 'something like the one we went to see in Elgin Cathedral, as far as we know. There are only three references to the Strathdonan Stone that I know of. One says that it was taller and broader than the Chieftain of Vannich, but we don't know which Chieftain.'

'It would be over six feet tall then,' I said. 'All the Somerleds in the portraits look enormous and I bet Somerled the Red was a giant.'

'The Macdonalds do run to height,' Aunt agreed and went on: 'and an old Gaelic story tells of an oath of which the words were: "I swear by the bearded saints on the Great Stone of St. Donan that stands in Strathdonan to avenge the blood of my brother."'

I shuddered. 'Aunt, you are almost too good at saying these old Highland things. You give me the creeps. If the third thing isn't nicer than that, don't say it.' She laughed. 'It's much nicer, though. It is a translation of an old Gaelic song, a song of the time before Somerled the Gambler gambled Strathdonan away, when everybody was happy and this was a lovely place. Any place is lovely to people who are happy in it. It is a love song and the young man is comparing his lady to all the most beautiful things he can think of, as young men in love always do. At one point he says:

She is the bright of the day when the saints bless Strathdonan
And rest on the house in the shade of their stone.
She is the peace of the night when the moon lights
                                                    Strathdonan
And the saints raise their prayers to God on His throne.

Aunt looked down into the glen where the sun was shining today and said: 'Either he was very much in love or she was a remarkably beautiful and fine young woman — maybe both. Anyway, the lover and his lass are dead and forgotten long ago except by a few musty old library-rakers like me and they are remembered by us only for the young man's reference to the Strathdonan Stone.' She looked up at the hill on our right again. 'I have always fancied that hilltop as the site of the Stone. If it stood on that hill, I believe that its shadow would have struck the roof of the house at noon. But I have been all over the top of that hill and there is not a trace. Come along, we'd better be on our way.'

'But what could *happen* to a great heavy stone of that size?' I asked as we drove down into the glen.

Aunt shrugged her shoulders. 'Lots of things. It could have fallen and been broken up to build with. In the old days, people had no interest in those early carved stones — they did not know their historical value. And, having at least one flat side, the stones were very useful for lintels and doorsteps and things. All very sad.'

'But you never know when another reference to the stone may turn up,' I said, to comfort her. 'Somebody may even find the stone itself.'

F

She smiled. 'Nothing is impossible. My goodness, they *have* improved this place!'

We were now on the shore of the little loch, looking across at the house. All the ivy had been stripped off the walls and they did not look dark any more, but rather silvery in the sunlight. It was all a frightful muddle and mess, of course, with scaffolding and ladders and piles of wood and a cement mixer lying about among all the small branches and chips of bark from the trees that had been felled. We had to leave the car about a hundred yards from the house because the tractors pulling away the felled trees had cut up the roadway so much with their heavy tyres.

Somerled, who was cutting branches off a felled tree with a big axe, saw us and came to meet us.

'Congratulations, Somerled,' Aunt said. 'I take back all my croakings about a bad bargain.'

'You mean that? Good!' He turned to me. 'How do you like it now, Shona?'

'It is going to be splendid,' I said, glad that he was quite himself again. Probably he had been cross because he was worried about Strathdonan, I thought.

'Any more trouble with mischief-makers?' Aunt asked.

'Not here, but part of the new wall at the graveyard was knocked down the other night.'

'The graveyard? How maddening! You can't very well keep a watch on that too.'

The work went on until about six o'clock, when the foresters and masons went away, and we all went into the house because the evening grew chilly. Inside, except for the room just to the left of the door, it was all as dreary as ever because Somerled was taking advantage of the good weather to get the outside work done and would do the inside of the house later. But the first room we had ever seen was now furnished as a sort of living-room with a big table in the middle of the floor, and the kitchen at the back had been cleaned enough to be used for cooking the food.

'The Camerons are still over at the graveyard,' Somerled said. 'Sit down, Liz. Will you stay for supper? It's all a bit rough, but we have trout. If Angus and Scott, the chauffeur, go on as they are doing, there won't be a trout left in the loch, and Moore, that secretary chap, is nearly as good with a rod as they are.'

Angus now came into the room and said: 'The Cameron gentlemen are very late tonight. They are not back from the church as yet, I notice.'

But, before any of us could say anything, the Land-Rover stopped outside and old Mr. Cameron came stamping into the room, obviously on the verge of having one of his fits. Mr. Fourth and Fifth came right behind him and Mr. Fourth said: 'Now, stop it, Dad. Going on like that won't get us anywheres. Sit down.'

'What has happened?' Aunt asked.

'This,' Mr. Fourth said, and, putting a bundle of sacking he was carrying on the table, he unrolled it and exposed a lot of broken-up black stuff, broken glass and cut-up leather. 'This is the remains of my camera and its case,' he said, and went on to explain that he had left the camera on the seat of the Land-Rover. 'When we were ready to come home, we found that,' he ended.

'But if anyone was about over there, you must have seen him!' Somerled said angrily.

Mr. Fourth shook his head. 'Didn't see a living being the whole afternoon except the masons and ourselves.'

'And you didn't hear anything? That lens must have

been hammered to pieces with a stone, and there is never a sound over there in the Broad Glen!' Somerled was angry, I knew, because the thing did not seem to make any sense. 'You can't tell me that that damage was done in silence!'

Mr. Fourth shook his head and Angus said in his quiet, thoughtful voice: 'There is no proof that the damage was done in the Broad Glen, Macdonald. The damager had the whole afternoon to do his work. I have known people about here who could move more quietly than a worm in the ground. Indeed, if Him That Used To Live Here were not dead and in his grave, I would suspect that he had crept up on you this afternoon.'

I felt shivery and stared at Angus, and I saw that Aunt was staring, too, with her eyes wide, but Somerled's eyes, instead of staring with fright, simply looked angrier as he said: 'Angus, what the blazes are you getting at?' He pointed at the debris on the sacking. 'That's not the work of a ghost!'

'I am not speaking of ghosts, Macdonald,' said Angus calmly. 'I am speaking of those who have the nature of the poacher in them.' He turned to old Mr. Cameron and his son. 'When I was a little younger, as the Macdonald will agree, I could have come to the Land-Rover on a bright day like this in the middle of the Broad Glen and have taken your camera away and have brought it back too, and I do not think you would have seen or heard me.'

'That is true enough,' Somerled agreed.

'But I would not have broken the camera. I was never one for breaking things,' said Angus. 'Now, the only one about here that I know of, now that Him That Used To Live Here is gone and myself is a little older, that can move like a real poacher is Kenny the Shepherd's oldest boy and this is not

Young Kenny's work, for he is not a destructive boy, although very wicked and mischievous at times. And, besides, has he not been with myself and under my own eye all this day, driving the tractor out there? — which he should not be doing and him too young to have a licence, but what the police do not know will not hurt them, the poor innocent creatures!' He looked at old Mr. Cameron. 'Now, there is a thing that I am noticing about all this destructiveness that we are having which I will tell you of, if you will be good enough not to get all excited and beyond yourself.'

'All right, I am listening,' old Mr. Cameron barked.

'At first, it seemed to be just destructiveness in general, but, of late, it seems to be more and more directed against your son here,' said Angus.

'My son? What the devil — !' old Mr. Cameron raised his stick and shook it, but Angus merely looked more calm than ever and said: 'Now put down that stick or it is myself will take it from you and put it on the fire. That is not the way to use a walking-stick whatever.'

'You know, Angus has got something,' Somerled said. 'Lately, it has been *all* your things, Fourth — your papers torn up, your coat in the loch and now your camera.' He turned to Angus. 'What do you suggest we do, Angus?'

'I think we should put Young Kenny over to the grave-yard with the gentlemen here. He should not be driving that tractor whatever, useful as he is.' Angus now spoke to the Camerons. 'You will not see Young Kenny, of course, but he will be there. It always needs a poacher to catch a poacher. Policemen are not any use at it. They are too heavy as a rule and their feet are too big. I am told that in the cities they are now going for smaller policemen that they hope have more brains, but up here we still have the old-fashioned sort. Any poacher worth the name standing in the courtyard at Castle Vannich could hear the sergeant leaving his station in Vannich Village, poor big honest fellow!'

Aunt, Somerled and I began to laugh at Angus's strangely upside-down attitude to honesty, dishonesty, policemen and the law in general while the Camerons looked bewildered, but they agreed to take his advice and have Young Kenny as their invisible watchman.

After our supper of delicious grilled trout, Aunt said: 'Are you coming back to Vannich tonight or tomorrow morning, Somerled?'

'Tomorrow is only Saturday,' he replied. 'I'm not coming over till Sunday morning.'

'Somerled, Miss Digby arrives tomorrow,' Aunt said, 'and I think you should be there to welcome her.'

'Film stars aren't my cup of tea,' said Somerled, sticking his chin out as he had done about welcoming the Camerons.

Aunt looked at Angus before she said: 'Now, look here, Somerled, don't let's have all this nonsense all over again. You are a hotel-keeper. You have to—'

'Come down to the lake, Shona,' Fifth said. 'I'll get my guitar. It sounds fabulous over the water.'

'You don't have to keep on telling me I'm a hotel-keeper!' Somerled said, getting angry. 'I know that, but I'm not going to be a flunkey to some old painted-up trout of a film star.'

Aunt sighed. 'Miss Digby is not old and she is not a film star. She is a singer who has made a great and sudden success and she must be a very hard-working young woman, but that is beside the point. She is bringing us a great deal of valuable publicity with this television show that she hopes to do from the castle, and the least you can do—'

'Oh, come *on*, Shona!' said Fifth.

'Aunt,' I said, 'is it *Dainty* Digby who is coming?'

'Yes,' said Aunt shortly to me and then: 'Now, Somerled—'

'No!' he said angrily. 'Welcome her yourself!'

'Oh, Somerled,' I said, 'she is absolutely fabulous. Somerled, you *must* be there! Why, most people would give their ears to talk to Dainty Digby. Gosh, when I go back to school and tell people that I have really *seen* her—'

'Would *you* like to talk to her?' Somerled asked me suddenly.

'Oh, no! I couldn't think of anything to say to a person like that.'

'Neither can I,' he said.

'Come on down to the lake, Shona,' Fifth said again, having now fetched his guitar.

Goodness, was I bored with that guitar! And he couldn't really play it for toffee, anyhow.

'Not tonight, Fifth,' I said and glared at Somerled. 'I am going back to the castle with Aunt. *Some* of us have got to remember that we keep an hotel and be there to welcome the guests.'

Somerled suddenly began to laugh. He was a little bit like Ben Vannich—he was covered in clouds and thunder one moment and all sparkle and sunlight the next, I thought.

'Get in the car, Shona,' he said. 'Drive back to the castle with me and brief me about Dainty Digby. If I have to talk to her, I had better know something about her.'

I told him all about Dainty Digby, about how she had suddenly come right to the top as a pop singer and had toured the United States and Australia and all sorts of places and been mobbed by fans at all the airports, and how, in Paris, she was known as 'la Petite' and everything.

'It's marvellous, her coming to our hotel,' I said. 'Gosh, when I go back to school, won't all their eyes pop out with envy! It will be even more thrilling than last year when Iain found the Vannich Jewel and his picture was in all the newspapers. And, Somerled, I must tell you again that I think the way you have displayed the White Hind and the Jewel in the Great Tower is splendid.'

'It was your aunt's idea really,' he said.

It was in connection with this that Somerled had called Aunt a genius as well as a Highland haybag on the night we arrived at the castle. When Iain found the lost Jewel and the White Hind in the secret room, we had regarded it as a private thing between us and the Macdonald family, but Iain's discovery leaked out and the next day the castle was swarming with news-reporters and masses of people arrived, asking to see the White Hind and the Jewel. It was then that Aunt had her genius idea and suggested that, instead of walling up the secret room again as he had intended to do, Somerled should take one wall *out* of it so that people could see into it from the top room of the Great Tower and now this had been done. About six feet up the wall in the top room, there was a big sheet of thick plate glass behind a wrought-iron grille and through these you could see the White Hind of Vannich standing guard over the jewelled crucifix which lay in a velvet box at her feet. What you could *not* see, as Somerled told me, was the burglar alarm that would wake the whole countryside if anyone tried to tamper with the grille or the plate-glass window.

When we arrived back at the castle and got out of the cars in the courtyard, I was still thinking about that evening the summer before when Somerled and I found Iain with the treasures in the secret room and then I remembered the house at Strathdonan. When we left it, the sun had gone round to the west and had reddened and now that the ivy was gone the walls had looked pinkish.

'Aunt,' I asked, 'are there any stories of lost treasure about Strathdonan?'

'Apart from the Celtic Stone,' she said, 'none that I know of.'

'So there are none, Shona,' Somerled said.

'Mind you, Gordon the Gambler, who won the place from Somerled the Gambler, was known as Gordon the Miser before he died, wasn't he, Angus?'

'That is so, but the meaning of it was that None of Them Who Used To Live Over There would pay their debts. They would not even pay the wages of their workpeople. Dead as they are, it has to be said that they were very dishonourable sort of men. I do not think that you will find any hidden treasure at Strathdonan, Shona.'

Aunt and Angus went away inside, and Somerled said to me: 'Can that Cameron chap really play that guitar, Shona?'

'No,' I said, 'not for peanuts.'

Somerled gave a loud laugh and I left him and went upstairs.

When my brothers were going to bed, we swopped news about the day, as we always do, and when I burst forth about Dainty Digby coming, Neil just said: 'Oh, pooh,' in a disgusted way and Donald said in his newspaper-quoting voice: 'The modern Cinderella has a fabulous wardrobe and jewels even more fabulous, but she is still a quiet, home-loving girl who likes her mother to go with her everywhere. Nowadays, of course, her dresser and her manager are also in the party.' He then added in his own voice: 'I wonder if they all sit round when she's in the bath?'

'Probably she doesn't have baths,' Neil said, trying to annoy me, but I took no notice.

'Wish I was Dainty Digby,' said Donald. 'Shona, I read about a French nobleman who never took a bath all his life. He said it weakened the spine.'

'You are not a French nobleman,' I said and pointed across the passage.

'Just think if my spine got weak and you were to blame. What a thing to have on your conscience!'

I merely went on pointing and when he went across to the bathroom I followed him, of course, to see that he washed. Neil came, too, and leaned against the wash-basin.

'Strathdonan is going to be rather nice after all,' I said then.

'It's going to be super,' said Neil. 'You could see that from the start. Somerled is nobody's fool, after all, Shona,' he said in old Mr. Cameron's voice and then, after a short pause: 'I thought of a thing today.'

I often wonder if other people feel about their brothers as I feel about mine. There are times when Neil and Donald are a bit of a bore because I seem to know them too well, so well that I even know what they are thinking before they say it. When Neil says: 'I thought of a thing' as he had said it now, it means that this thing he has thought of is a thing that is absolutely bang-on for Neil, and he is either going to try to borrow money or try to persuade you to do something that he specially wants and you don't.

'What?' I said, feeling on guard.

'I think it's a shame how we always spend Christmas at home having fun and poor Aunt is at Jennyville all alone.'

This made me more suspicious than ever. First of all, it is ridiculous for anybody to refer to Aunt as 'poor Aunt,' especially Neil or Donald or I, for Aunt is one of those people who do not need company, especially the company of Neil or Donald or me. I think she quite likes us, you know, and would not like us to be ill or miserable or anything, but, for company, she would rather have some musty old book about the Highland Clearances, and Neil knows this as well as I do, so I waited for what he would say next.

'When we go home,' he said, 'let's get to work about spending the whole Christmas holidays with Aunt. After all, we know about Santa Claus now,' he added in a sarcastic voice. 'It would be much more in the spirit of Christmas to come to Aunt and cheer her up than staying at home having Christmas stockings.'

Neil goes too far sometimes and now even Donald, sitting in the bath without his glasses, was blinking at his smug voice talking about the spirit of Christmas and cheering Aunt up.

'After all,' I said in a voice as sarcastic as his had been, 'Aunt knows about Santa Claus, too. *She* doesn't believe in him either any more. And she certainly wouldn't believe in the three of us, all full of the Christmas spirit, coming to cheer her up. Aunt is nobody's fool, after all, Neil,' I said in Mr. Cameron's voice and then: 'Neil Cameron, why do you want to come up here at Christmas?'

'Actually,' he said, looking surprised as if, that very second, the idea had dawned on him, 'if we were with Aunt at Christmas, we could all go to Strathdonan and learn to ski.'

'I'm in favour,' said Donald. 'Camerons calling and repeating: "I'm in favour."'

'So am I,' I admitted, 'but look, Neil, the wrap-around about the spirit of Christmas and cheering Aunt up won't do. We've got to think of something better before we tackle the parents.'

'Any ideas?' he asked.

'No.'

'My mind feels utterly obstacled,' said Donald.

'As long as we are all agreed, we are bound to think of something,' Neil said.

It was now that I remembered about Mr. Fourth's camera being all broken up and I told the boys about the plan of Young Kenny mounting guard.

'Angus says it takes a poacher to catch a poacher,' I said.

'Donald,' said Neil in a dramatic voice, 'tomorrow you can get along without me. I am going right over there to mount guard with Young Kenny.'

'Me, too,' said Donald, getting out of the bath, tripping over his slipper and sitting down on his behind with a thump.

'Between us, Kenny and I will collar him!' said Neil, striking a dramatic attitude and knocking over a tumbler which smashed in the wash-basin.

'I'm coming too!' said Donald from the floor.

'Neither of you is going,' I said. 'Neil makes too much noise and you are too clumsy. Get up and dry yourself. From now on, nobody is going to the graveyard except the Camerons and the masons and Young Kenny.'

'Then I'll go to Strathdonan and drive the tractor,' said Neil.

'Me too,' said Donald.

'Are you lot going to bed tonight or tomorrow?' Aunt asked in the doorway and so we went to bed.

6. The Mischief-maker
Becomes Visible

THE next day, a tremendous number of visitors came to
the tea-room and the gardens and museum, far more
than we had ever had before on a summer Saturday. And
they did not simply visit and go away as they usually do.
They hung around the courtyard, the Great Yett and the
north drive and when we were at lunch, Aunt said: 'It
seems incredible, but they are all waiting to gape at this
unfortunate young woman. I think it rather a shame that
they can't leave her to have her holiday in peace.'

'What young woman?' Neil asked.

'This Miss Digby who is coming,' she told him and then:
'Shona, if you don't mind, you had better put on a cap and
apron this afternoon and give a hand in the tea-room. More
people are arriving every second.'

'But I want to see Dainty Digby, too!' I protested.

'You will have lots of opportunity. There is no need to gape in the courtyard. She is to be here for a fortnight.'

During the forenoon, I had been looking forward as much as anybody to seeing Dainty Digby, but as the afternoon wore on and more and more people gathered outside I began to feel that it was all a bit silly, all these fat ladies standing in the hot sun waiting to see this girl who was only about three years older than I was. And when I saw Somerled, looking very handsome, go over to the Stirrup Stone followed by Angus and four of the gardeners, who began to move the people back from the Great Yett, I felt it was sillier still. And then the car came into the courtyard and it was really a bit frightening and I felt sorry for Dainty Digby, for the crowd went surging round it — the gardeners could not keep them back — as it crawled towards the main door under the Great Tower.

I had been looking through the window of the tea-room and now I discovered that I was quite alone. All the girls and Miss Smiley too had joined the crowd outside and I felt sort of angry. After all, I thought, I am Aunt's niece and I've got shares in this hotel and I have as much right to see Dainty Digby as any of these people. So I tore out on to the west lawn, ran round the outside of the Great Tower, in through the dining-room on the south front and arrived inside the main door just as Somerled was handing Dainty Digby out of the car and leading her inside.

From the moment she set foot inside the castle, everything started to go wrong. Standing beside Somerled, she looked very tiny and dainty and her little feet in their high-heeled shoes made me feel that my feet in my sandals were as flat as flounders and absolutely enormous. But as well as looking tiny and dainty she also looked very cross. She looked round, frowning, at Aunt, Angus, Miss Dotty, Miss Coocoo, the receptionist and all of us, and then said: 'Is nobody here?' I could not think what she meant and so I looked at Aunt, but she, too, looked completely at sea until the manager man came forward and murmured something to her.

'Oh, the Press?' Aunt said then and laughed. 'Oh, yes. We have incarcerated them in a room upstairs. You need not see them, Miss Digby, unless you wish.'

Miss Digby glared scornfully at Aunt as if she were an idiot, and said: 'Of *course* I want to see them!' and then she turned to Somerled.

'Where do we go?'

As if he were mesmerised, Somerled led her away; the manager, the dresser and her mother fell in behind, and they were hardly out of the room when Aunt exploded: 'The swelled-headed, conceited, over-dressed under-mannered little brat!'

'Now then, Elizabeth——' Angus began.

'For two pins I'd turn her up and smack her bottom!' said Aunt.

'You must remember that you are a hotel-keeper now, as you are always reminding the Macdonald,' said Angus.

'For two pins——' Aunt was beginning again, when Miss Coocoo gave her tinkling silvery laugh and said: 'How *too* extraordinary—don't you think?—that somebody should *look* at one and then *tell* one that one is *nobody*!'

'Bah!' said Miss Dotty, and Aunt turned to me and said snappily: 'Go back to the tea-room and feed all these silly women outside! And if I catch you gaping at that young woman and making her head more swollen than it is already, I'll turn *you* up and smack *your* bottom!'

'Now, Elizabeth, Shona's bottom is not in the matter,'
Angus began, but I did not stay any longer. There are times
when it is safer to be out of Aunt's sight.

When I got back to the tea-room all the girls were pop-
eyed and phrases like 'Absolutely fabulous' and 'Simply
dreamy' were flying about, and I was quite glad when the
huge crowd of people came surging in for tea and we were
all too busy to speak at all, but, when the rush was over, all
the girls gathered in a huddle and began to look forward to
the dance that evening.

There was dancing after dinner for the guests every evening in the ballroom, but on Saturday evenings the student
workers could join in the dance too if they wanted to. I had
never thought of going to the dances because I have never
danced much except at school parties, and all the other
holiday-job girls were older than I was and had boy-friends
to take them to the dance. Usually, on Saturday evenings
when it was fine, I went around with Fifth and my brothers
or for a row on the loch with one of the ghillies and sometimes Somerled came too, but on this evening Somerled had
dinner with Dainty Digby and her party, and then they all
went away through to the ballroom. And Angus went away
to the private sitting-room with Miss Dotty and Miss Coocoo; Fifth went out for a drive with his people; and Aunt
went frowning away to her office, which left Neil and
Donald and me at a loose end and staring at one another.
I am really very fond of Neil and Donald, but, on this evening, they both seemed terribly young and silly, so I left them
and went mooning out for a walk along the side of the loch.

It was a beautiful evening and on fine evenings when the
sun goes to the west Loch Vannich turns to gold and all
round about are the trees, then the heathery hills and, tower-

ing all over all, the peak of Ben Vannich. I love this place
and, as a rule, when you are in a place you love you feel
happy, but on this evening as I walked along the shore of
the loch I felt absolutely miserable. I felt that I was exactly
the wrong age to fit in with anybody or anything. I was too
old to play around with Neil and Donald, and although
Fifth was about my age, his background was too different
from mine for him to be comfortable company and, besides,
he was such a bore with that guitar of his. And then I was
too young to be real friends with Aunt, to be the sort of
person she would confide in properly. She had exploded
about Dainty Digby that afternoon because she was so angry,
but now she would not talk about her at all. And I was too
young, and felt I didn't dance well enough, to go to the
dance in the ballroom and, in any case, I could not possibly
go alone, without a partner.

At last, I went back to Aunt's office, for at least she was
company and not silly like the boys, but when I got there I
found the room empty, so there was nothing for it but to
go upstairs to my own room. As I went up the main staircase, I could hear the music coming from the ballroom and,
from the landing, I saw that the little door to the gallery
above the ballroom was open. This first floor is where the
guest bedrooms are, and Aunt does not allow Neil, Donald
or me to go along the passages. We are supposed to go
straight on from the landing up the corkscrew stairs to our
own rooms, which were the old nurseries, but on this evening
I decided I would go along to the gallery and look for a
short while at the people dancing down below. I ran along,
close to the wall, on tiptoe as one does when doing something
one shouldn't, and had to pull up short outside the door
when I heard Aunt's voice inside saying: 'I don't like it,

G

Angus. I wish I had let him stay at Strathdonan. This is a real Macdonald plunge.'

'You brought him here for the best, Elizabeth,' said Angus's quiet voice, 'and it will all come right in the end.'

I was just going to run back to the landing when Aunt came out of the gallery and saw me.

'Were you looking for me, Shona?' she asked.

'I was, sort of and then I saw the gallery door and—'

'You wanted to see the dancing?' She smiled, as if asking me to forgive her for being cross that afternoon. 'All right. Come in. Angus and I were watching, too.'

I had been in here and had looked down into the ballroom before, but it had been empty then. Now, filled with people swirling about among the music, it looked beautiful, and right underneath us I saw Somerled's red-gold hair shining in the lights from the chandeliers. It was odd in a way to look down at the tops of all these heads and realise that the people below were quite unaware of being watched from above, for none of them and least of all Somerled thought of looking up. He was too busy looking down at Dainty Digby's fair hair, which was a good way under his chin, and the way he held her reminded me a little of how Father used to hold my brothers when they were babies, very tenderly and carefully, as if he were afraid he would bruise or break them.

I suddenly wished I had never come to the gallery at all and said: 'How silly they all look from up here, Aunt, like fish goggling round and round at the bottom of a pond.'

'They *do* look pretty silly,' she agreed, 'but I suppose the whole world would look pretty silly if you saw it from Mars, goggling round and round the sun like a goldfish. Let's get off upstairs, shall we?'

I did not go to have my usual bed-time chat with my brothers. I went off to bed with my book, but I could not read it for thinking of Somerled and Dainty Digby. I wanted Somerled to be happy and have what he wanted and every-thing, but, at the same time, I had a horrid feeling that, now, nothing at Castle Vannich would ever be the same again, and it was all such a muddle that eventually I cried into my pillow until I must have fallen asleep.

The next day, Somerled seemed to have turned into quite a different person. He did not seem even to notice any of us, not even his best friend, Angus. He seemed to be able to see nobody except Dainty Digby. He did not do any of his usual Sunday things, like going to church or taking his motor-boat on to the loch. He simply disappeared after break-fast and was not seen again until about eleven o'clock, when he came downstairs with Dainty Digby and they both got into his car and drove away. They were not back when I went to bed that night, and the next morning he did not go off to Strathdonan, but simply disappeared after breakfast and was not seen again until about eleven o'clock, when he came downstairs with Dainty Digby and they both got into —I know that this sounds like a gramophone record that has got stuck and I have made it sound like that on purpose, for that is exactly how it seemed, as if Somerled had got into a groove that led nowhere except round and round Dainty Digby.

And Somerled being like this and not like his former self made everybody else different too. Aunt was cross and snappy, and Miss Dotty, who was usually very quiet, stamped about, making a noise, while talkative, fluttery Miss Coocoo did not say a word and hardly moved.

After a few days of this, Angus was having breakfast with

Aunt, my brothers and me and Aunt said: 'Let's get into the car and go over to Strathdonan. *Some*body has to take some interest in the work over there or it will never be ready for the winter season. Donald, stop champing at that cereal like a horse eating hay!' she ended angrily.

Donald looked startled until Angus said: 'Let the boy be, Elizabeth. That stuff he is eating is very noisy stuff. And it is not the fault of any of us at this table that the work at Strathdonan is being neglected.'

'Sorry, Angus,' said Aunt as she got up. 'Eat a big breakfast, Donald. I'll arrange a picnic lunch and I'll meet you all in the courtyard at half past nine.'

'What's the matter with Aunt, Angus?' Donald asked when she had gone. 'Has she got a headache?'

'Everybody's got a headache, Muggins,' said Neil, 'because Somerled's in love. Love, phooey!' and he put his thumbs in his ears, waggled his fingers and gave a loud wail.

'Stop that, Neil Cameron!' I said. 'My goodness, you are fourteen years old. Besides, you don't know what you're talking about.'

Neil got furious. 'I know enough to know that it's all rot about finding them under gooseberry bushes, Smarty. Crumbs, that Dainty Digby! She *smells*!'

'Neil Cameron!' I said and could not find the words to go any farther. I was really loving Neil for being horrible about Dainty Digby, but, of course, I could not admit that.

'It's that perfume of hers,' Donald said and, holding a forkful of bacon, he gazed through his glasses at the portrait of Somerled the Scholar on the far wall and said in his newspaper-quoting voice: 'Specially created for her in Paris, it is called reeve dee lah pea tight.'

'What a very strange name for a smell!' said Angus.

'Called *what*?' I asked in the same moment.

'Reeve dee la pea tight,' Donald repeated through the mouthful of bacon. 'That's what it said in the magazine at Mother's hairdresser's.'

'Spell it,' said Neil, and Donald spelled out the letters he had read with which Neil and I both said: 'Reve de la Petite!' and I explained: 'It's French, Donald.'

'What does it mean?'

'Dream of the little girl,' I said.

Donald put down his fork altogether, looked at me solemnly through his glasses and said sternly, quoting Father: 'If you don't know a thing, Shona, say so. There is no shame in not knowing, but it is shamefully stupid to pretend to a knowledge you have not got.'

He returned to his own voice: 'How can a dream of a little girl or even of a big girl be a smell?' he asked. 'Don't be dopey!'

Father says that talking to Donald sometimes is to have your mind anaesthetised by too-pure reason, and I felt that my mind was anaesthetised now and was grateful when Angus said: 'Donald, if you are finished eating for the present, we had better make ready to meet your aunt, for she is not in the mood these days to be kept waiting.'

Aunt and I sat in the front of the car, but she was very quiet, and Angus and the boys in the back did not talk much either, although, as a rule, Neil and Donald talk all the time, especially when they are with Angus, because he can tell them so many interesting things. When we had passed through Vannich Village and came to the turning inland along the shore of the river, we saw Findlay Elton walking along, and Aunt stopped, and smiled for the first time that day.

'Hello, Findlay,' she said, 'would you like to come in the car with us?'

Findlay looked round at us all, smiling, and then he nodded his head vigorously.

'Come close to me, Shona, and let him come in beside you.'

When we started off again, we were still quiet, but it was a different sort of quietness — the quietness of Findlay's pleasure at having a car ride.

'You like the car, don't you, Findlay?' I asked, and he nodded again, not taking his eyes off the front of the bonnet, and so I looked there too and discovered that there was something magical in the way the road seemed to slide towards the car and under it, as if the road and not the car were moving. Probably, I concluded, this is what Findlay thought was happening and that when you got into a car, some magic made the road slide under and past you.

Quite soon, we came to the turning where the road left the riverside and forked for Strathdonan, and when Aunt turned to the left instead of going straight on up the Broad Glen, Findlay began to shout: 'No, no, no!' and tried to open the car door. I grabbed at his hand, but he threw me away roughly so that I fell back against Aunt and she at once stood on the brakes and the car jerked to a stop as Findlay threw the door open and hurled himself out on to the grass at the roadside. When he scrambled to his feet, his face was white and his eyes were big and frightened, so Aunt and I got out and went to him. Aunt put an arm round his shoulders and said: 'What is the matter, Findlay? What scared you?' He pointed ahead to where the road went over the brow of the hill into Strathdonan and said: 'Bad! Bad place. Not go!' and he wriggled free of Aunt's arm and ran away back towards the river. Aunt and I stood looking after him and now Angus came out of the car and said: 'He will be all right, Elizabeth. He will come to no harm.'

Aunt looked up the road towards Strathdonan and said: 'But, Angus, what did he mean? Why should Findlay with his injured mind think of Strathdonan as a bad place?'

'It would be hard to know what may be in a mind that has suffered as much as poor Findlay's. Come now, Elizabeth, and do not upset yourself about the boy. He will come to no harm in the glen.' Aunt gave a little shiver, got back into the car, and drove on.

Now we were all quieter than ever, and I thought that this certainly was one of those days when everything goes wrong. Then when we went over the brow of the hill and down into Strathdonan, the sun disappeared and everything became gloomy, and I looked down at the house, dark, sombre, grey in the clouded light, hearing again Findlay's voice saying: 'Bad! Bad place.'

When we reached the house and got out of the car, I did not go off exploring with the boys, but stuck close to Aunt and Angus while they talked to the workmen and looked at the progress that had been made. It was all strangely different from the evening when we had had supper here with Somerled. It seems silly when you say it, but it was as if this house had a sad, sullen spirit that only the presence of Somerled could overcome, and today it felt as if it did not want any of us, as if it resented us as intruders and wanted to be left alone to brood over its dark thoughts in this deserted glen.

And yet it should have looked more cheerful than ever before, because the painters were working in the old part, making the ceiling of the first room we had seen a beautiful blue and picking out the plaster garlands in white, and, in the newer L-shaped wing, joiners were sawing and hammering and tearing up the rotten floorboards, but the old drawing-room with the tattered curtains was as dreary and musty as ever. The master joiner said they were leaving it until the very last because, if there was not time to do it before the winter, it would be shut off altogether and done up when the ski-ing season was over.

'Quite a good idea, I suppose,' Aunt said, looking round it. Then she drew her shoulders in and shivered. 'But I hope you can get it done in time. It is horrible as it is. It feels like a burial vault.'

I was glad to go outside and walk down to the side of the loch with Aunt and Angus. The sun had come out again, making the water sparkle, and we went to sit near the broken stone jetty that ran out into the water.

'The Macdonald should have that jetty blasted away for safety's sake,' Angus said. 'It should never have been built in the first of it. It is a dirty, dangerous thing. It was here that Gordon the Miser met his end, and I have heard it said that it was eleven days before they found the body.'

In spite of the sun, I felt cold. There seemed to be no spot in this glen that was not haunted by tragedy.

'Aunt,' I said, to change the subject to something I found more pleasant, 'what did you mean when you said that Findlay had an injured mind? Wasn't he born with an incomplete brain like Ninkie?' In the family, we refer to my brother Iain as Ninkie, but Angus, of course, always calls him by his proper name, Iain.

'No, Shona,' Aunt said. 'Findlay is not the same kind of person as Ninkie. Findlay was originally merely a little mentally slow and backward, but he had a very cruel father who hated him, and that made Findlay much worse.'

I wished now that I had never spoken about Findlay, it was so horrifying, but a thought struck me and I blurted out: 'But how could a sweet person like Mrs. Elton have a horrible, cruel son like Findlay's father?'

'Findlay is Mrs. Elton's daughter's child, Shona. He is called Findlay Elton because his grandmother does not want him to have his father's name and I don't blame her.'

'Have you got any further with that business, Elizabeth?' Angus asked.

'Not a bit, Angus. Mrs. Elton can't make up her mind, poor old soul.'

'What business?' I asked, risking a snub. 'Is it to do with Findlay?' I felt sort of fierce and protective about Findlay, very much as I feel about my brother Iain, for people like Findlay and Iain have to have people to protect them. Aunt did not snub me. Instead, she smiled in her nicest way, a smile that is mostly in her eyes.

'There is no harm in your knowing, Shona,' she said, 'but there isn't much to know. Mrs. Elton has found out that Findlay's father died recently. She pretended for a long time that he died long ago, but it was only her daughter, Findlay's mother who died. The father died quite recently. She confessed this to me that day we all went to see her. She wanted to ask me whether she should make a claim on the father's estate for Findlay. Angus and I both think that she should but—'

'Of course she should!' I interrupted. 'If that horrible man left anything at all, Findlay should have it!'

Aunt smiled again. 'But Mrs. Elton isn't sure that she wants anything of his for Findlay. Mrs. Elton is a Highlander from the west and such people can think in a way even more unusual than ordinary Highlanders like Angus and me. She says that this man's money, if there is any, may be tainted and would do Findlay more harm than good.'

'Nonsense!' I said. 'You and Angus should go ahead on your own and get whatever there is for Findlay. Then he could be properly looked after when Mrs. Elton is too old, don't you see?'

'Angus and I can see,' said Aunt, making me realise that I had been a bit opinionated, but she was not annoyed, as she went on: 'and we would do exactly what you say, only we don't know this man's name or when or where he died, except that Mrs. Elton let out that it was somewhere in England and fairly recently.'

'Aunt,' I said, 'I am not trying to be too big for my boots, but would you let *me* have a go at Mrs. Elton about this? Maybe I could make her see by telling her about Nink and everything.'

Aunt stared at me until Angus said very quietly: 'It can do no harm, Elizabeth. It never does any harm to let true feeling have its say and Shona feels truly about this boy.'

'All right, Shona,' Aunt said. 'One day soon, you, Angus and I will go and call on Mrs. Elton. Now, run and find the boys. Mr. Fourth is meeting us at the fork with the Land-Rover and we are going up to the old church to have lunch with him and the others.'

The joiners told me that Neil and Donald had gone into the wood behind the house, a very black, sinister place where the trees had been left to make a windbreak on the north side. I did not feel like pushing my way through all the tangled underbrush, so I made the loud hallooing noise that is the Cameron call and Neil and Donald answered me from the thick darkness. It was not long before they came crashing out and ran towards me, very excited, Neil shouting: 'Shona,

look what we found in the wood! Mr. Fourth's field-glasses that were stolen. They were hanging on the branch of a tree.'

It was the pleasantest thing of that day up till then to drive to the fork in the road and give the field-glasses back to Mr. Fourth, and then Aunt left her car at the roadside and we all got into the Land-Rover and bumped over the rough track to the old church.

I remembered the first time I had seen this place, all lonesome and desolate and rather eerie, the ruins of the church standing alone among the tall trees in the middle of the glen, but now it looked quite different. One wall of the churchyard was completely built, the others partly built, and the tall pillars for the gates were in place. It gave you a feeling that perhaps the people who had been buried here long ago might know that old Mr. Cameron thought of them, and that this might be of some comfort to them. But when I told him how splendid I thought his wall looked, he frowned in his cross way and looked dissatisfied.

'I don't like a graveyard with no graves and no people around to walk in it sometimes and think of those that are gone,' he said. 'It's the ghost of a graveyard and in my book ghosts don't make any sense.'

He suddenly turned to Aunt. 'Look here, Miss Cameron, you know what that young fellah should do? He should go in for a proper development around here.'

'Somerled?' Aunt asked. 'Somerled and the rest of us have no capital left for further development.'

Mr. Cameron took no notice of what she said. He did not ever take notice of anything when his mind was set on something else.

'We got the sites of all these old crofts on our aerial pictures, haven't we? What that young fellah should do is put a little holiday chalet on the site of every one of 'em and then he would really be in the ski-holiday business.'

'He doesn't want to do any such thing,' said Aunt fiercely, 'and don't you go giving him any ideas that will make him any more foolish than he is already.'

'That young fellah is nobody's fool,' said Mr. Cameron, shaking his stick, and I heard Aunt say, under her breath to Angus as she unpacked the picnic: 'In my book Somerled Macdonald is the biggest fool in Ross-shire this very minute.'

But Aunt's argument with Mr. Cameron was interrupted by a shout from high up, behind the ruins of the church.

'Hi, you!' said the voice, and when I looked I saw Young Kenny swinging down a tall tree from branch to branch like a monkey and then dropping to the ground. There was a scrambling and a crashing among the brambles and briers behind the church, and old Mr. Cameron hurried round one side while Mr. Fourth and the boys ran round the other.

'Young Kenny's got the culprit!' Aunt said delightedly, but then Findlay Elton, carrying Mr. Fourth's brief-case, which had been laid as bait, ran out into the open, saw old Mr. Cameron, and stopped. The old man, of course, raised that stick of his and rushed forward shouting: 'Got you this time, you young devil!' and Aunt's shout of 'Don't! Put that stick down!' was too late.

Findlay's eyes became wide with terror; he dropped the case and ran away along the track, faster than you would believe any human being could run.

'Oh, you and that confounded stick!' said Aunt, and she jumped into the Land-Rover but she only switched the engine on and then off again. 'It's no good,' she said. 'He would only run all the harder if I chased him. Let's have lunch and then get down to the village. Findlay will go home to his grandmother.'

The three Camerons from Canada were looking at her in amazement and old Mr. Cameron said: 'Look, what's going on around here?' He turned to Young Kenny. 'Here you, why didn't you chase that guy and collar him?'

'It's only Findlay,' Young Kenny explained. 'You can't chase poor Findlay.' He looked disgustedly at the Camerons. '*Days* of the tractor-driving I have lost and it's only Findlay!' he said.

'What d'you mean only Findlay and—'

'Now, wait a minute, Father,' said Mr. Fourth. 'Yes, Miss Cameron?'

'The boy Findlay is mentally backward,' Aunt explained, 'but I have never known him be malicious before as he has been with you, Mr. Fourth.'

'Findlay is very full of maliciousness to some people,' Young Kenny said, 'but they keep out of his way and take no notice.'

'Now then, Young Kenny,' said Angus sternly, 'just you be good enough to explain yourself. I have never heard a bad word about Findlay.'

'Ach, people do not mention it,' Young Kenny said, 'for it would only worry his granny and Findlay cannot help it.'

'Just you tell me at once the name of anybody that Findlay has been malicious to before,' said Angus, still speaking very sternly.

'My own father is one of them,' Young Kenny said. 'At the lambing time, my father cannot leave his bag with his dinner in it anywhere in the glen but Findlay throws it into the river. Murdo the Roadman is another. Findlay is for ever cutting the tyres of his bicycle. And Jamie the Keeper and Ian Ross the Joiner and—'

'Very good, Young Kenny, that will do,' Angus said. 'I believe the truth of what you are saying. You go now with the boys here and have some picnic dinner while the rest of us discuss what is to be done. And then you can go back to Strathdonan and *not* drive that tractor, although I am sure that you will do it just the same.'

'Come, Shona,' Angus said to me and led me, Aunt, Mr. Cameron and Mr. Fourth round the corner of the new wall. He then looked at Mr. Fourth and said: 'You are not a bad-looking man, but it happens that you are unfortunate in your appearance with regard to Findlay.'

He then turned to old Mr. Cameron. 'You will kindly lean on that stick and have a little patience while I make an explanation,' he said in his sternest voice, and the old man decided to keep quiet.

'Findlay Elton is not a bad boy,' Angus went on, 'but he was born a little backward in his mind. But, worse than that, his father was cruel to him because of his backwardness and this made him worse than he need have been, poor lad. Still, he is a lot better than he was when he first came here with his granny two years ago, not a little because of the interest Miss Cameron has taken in him. When he first came here he was frightened of everybody except his granny and *you*—' he looked at old Mr. Cameron—'have undone a lot of good work today with that stick of yours, but, of course, you were not to know the position, although it is my own opinion that you are far too handy with that stick.' Angus turned again to Mr. Fourth. 'You heard Young Kenny tell me of the other men that Findlay does mischief to? Well, there is a thing that came to me while Young

Kenny was speaking. All these men are tall, dark-haired men of about your own age and —' he looked at Aunt now —'I would think that Findlay's father was a man of about the same age and appearance.' He turned back to Mr. Fourth. 'You have lost your camera and a few other odds and ends, but you will just have to comfort yourself that you are paying for another man's sin, that is all. You must not think of punishing Findlay for what he has done. The Macdonald ladies, the Macdonald, Miss Cameron and I will not allow any harm to come to Findlay or any worry to come to his granny.'

'Well,' said old Mr. Cameron, 'if that ain't telling us!'

'Yes,' said Mr. Fourth, 'Angus is telling us and what he is telling us makes sense to me. And what he told you about that stick makes sense too. Apart from this Findlay boy, you know what the doctors said.'

'Doctors!' said old Mr. Cameron. 'But look here, what a terrible thing about that boy!' He looked over to where Fifth was lying on the grass with Young Kenny, Neil and Donald. 'How come a man can be cruel to his own son? I don't get that. But can anything be done for the boy?' he asked Aunt.

'Not a great deal,' she said. 'He will always be backward, but with love and care he can be made happy and, in time, he could be a gardener —'

'Or a poacher,' smiled Angus.

'— and be quite a useful citizen,' Aunt ended.

Old Mr. Cameron continued to stare, frowning, at his own healthy grandson. 'If a little money would be of any use to this old granny of his,' he said, 'I have a dollar or two I'm not using at the moment.'

'I may take you up on that,' Aunt said, 'and thank you.

Mrs. Elton may need a little money for lawyer's fees.'

'Just let me know,' he said and stared across the glen beyond the new walls to where the croft houses had once stood. 'I am considering investing a few dollars around these parts, anyways, if that young fellah is agreeable, and I would invest a little in Findlay—' he looked at Angus, his old eyes not cross but twinkling '—by way of showing that I know I am a lucky man with sons and grandchildren who can hold their own in the world and are not scared of an old fool with a stick.'

Angus smiled, and Aunt said: 'Let's have lunch. I'd like to get down to Findlay's home.'

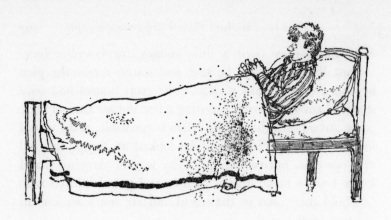

7. *A Lost Voice Calls*

As soon as lunch was over, Aunt arranged for Neil and Donald to stay at the old church with the Camerons, and Mr. Fourth drove her, Angus and me down to Aunt's car at the fork.

'I want to see Findlay as soon as possible,' she explained. 'The object is to make him forget you and your father, Mr. Fourth, and remember people like Shona and Angus that he isn't afraid of.'

Mrs. Elton came out of her cottage and was at her garden gate before Aunt stopped the car. She must have been waiting for us to come back through the village.

'Findlay's had a fright, Miss Cameron,' she said, her blue eyes all worried.

'I know,' Aunt said. 'I'll tell you about it later. Where is he? Do you think he will see any of us?'

'I am sure he will see *you*, Miss Cameron. He is in bed.' She spoke to Angus and me now. 'Findlay always goes to bed when he is afraid. He feels safe in bed, you see.' She turned to Aunt again. 'He has been worrying about you. He kept saying: "Bad place. Miss Cameron not go."'

'He means Strathdonan. He knew I went there this morning. Ask him if he will see me or Shona or Angus, Mrs. Elton.'

We stood in the little hall while Mrs. Elton went into Findlay's room, and we heard her say: 'Miss Cameron has come to see you, Findlay,' and after a little pause we heard Findlay say: ''iss Ca'eron?' thoughtfully as if he were trying to think what the words meant, and then: ''iss Ca'eron! 'iss Ca'eron!' in an excited and pleased tone. Mrs. Elton beckoned to Aunt to come into the room and Angus and I stood listening.

'Hello, Findlay,' Aunt said. 'Why are you in bed? Are you sick?'

'Not sick. See bad 'an. No bad 'an in bed.'

'No bad men anywhere,' Aunt said.

'Bad 'an. Bad place,' Findlay insisted.

After a little, Angus and I went in and talked to him too, and he became quite calm and even laughed a little, but he would not come out of bed, because he was sure that the 'bad 'an' was waiting to catch him.

Mrs. Elton insisted on going to make a cup of tea for us, and when she had left the room, Aunt whispered to me: 'Go and help her, Shona. And talk to her. Now is your chance when she is worried about Findlay.'

So I followed through to the little scullery whose window looked northwards over the Firth. I did not try to be tactful or wrap things up as Neil tries to do sometimes, and now I simply said straight out: 'Mrs. Elton, I hope you don't mind, but Aunt told me about Findlay's father being so cruel to him and everything. She has told me *all* about Findlay and about how his father had died and may have left some money and how you feel you ought not to claim it.'

Mrs. Elton stood with a plate of biscuits in her hand, staring at me with worried, puzzled eyes, not saying anything.

'You should claim that money if there is any,' I said. 'As Angus says, a thing like money cannot be good or bad. Only people are good or bad. Findlay's father was a bad man, but his money is just like any other money and could buy things that would be good for Findlay.'

She put down the plate of biscuits on the table and went on looking at me, saying nothing. 'My baby brother Iain — Aunt has told you about him — is a much more serious case than Findlay,' I went on: 'Iain was born with part of his brain missing, but he goes to a special school now and can do all sorts of things. If you got this money, supposing there is any, you could live in a place within reach of the kind of school Findlay needs, don't you see?'

She just went on looking at me. 'Mrs. Elton, Neil, Donald and I have a special fund for Iain — a box and we put in as much as we can to buy things for him, special things that he needs at school. We don't have to do this, but we do it because we want to help Iain, for we love him. And last week we made a box for Findlay, too, and it has nearly ten shillings in it already. We will help you, Mrs. Elton, and old Mr. Cameron from Canada will help you — *every*body will help you, but you have to help, too, by claiming Findlay's rights for him when he can't do it for himself.'

I had gone and got myself all worked up about this thing, for I felt that Aunt had some sort of faith in me about it, and I did not want to disappoint her, and, besides, I was so full of hate for this father of Findlay's that I wanted to grab any horrible money he had left because I was sure that his ghost would be furious at Findlay having it or something. Anyhow, I was so busy dancing about and banging the table with my fists and arguing against the silence of Mrs. Elton that, when I stopped speaking, I was astounded and horrified to see that she was crying, and more horrified still when she sat down, put her arms on the table, her head on her arms, and began to sob and sob.

'Oh,' I said. 'I'm sorry. I'll fetch Aunt.'

'No, don't,' she said, reaching out a hand and holding my arm. 'I am all right. It was you and your box for Findlay. I am all right.' She looked up at me with her wet, blue eyes. 'I will claim that money, if he left any, for Findlay, Shona,' she said, and I felt that I was going to burst with sheer happiness.

'Oh, dear,' I said, 'look at the kettle!' and I grabbed the thing, which was boiling over all over the stove. 'I'll make the tea. You sit still and get calmed down.' But I was not very calm myself. I felt I was boiling over like the kettle. 'I bet that horrible man left scads of money!' I said. 'I bet he won the football pools or something just before he died. You and Findlay will be able to live in Aberdeen or Edinburgh or Glasgow or London or wherever the best school for Findlay is and come up here for all the holidays. You will be able to—'

I had just overflowed the teapot and spilled water all over the floor when Aunt appeared in the doorway.

'Shona,' she said, 'for pity's sake, what are you going on about? You sound like a demented wireless set and look at that mess — !'

'You let her alone,' Mrs. Elton said, 'Miss Cameron, will you ask the Macdonald to call and see me? The Macdonald has been very good to me and my boy, and I owe it to him to discuss things with him first.'

Aunt's eyes sort of bulged. 'You mean you are going to claim — ? '

'Yes,' Mrs. Elton said, and gave a little sob. 'When so many people are so good to the boy, his granny must do what she can. I have been very stupid about it until now, until Shona explained it to me. Oh, I know that you and Angus tried to explain to me, but maybe I need the special sort of explaining that Shona can do, like Findlay needing to go to a special school. Shona, you carry the biscuits and I'll take the tray.'

On the way home to the castle, Aunt and Angus were more like their real selves than they had been since Dainty Digby came to stay, and I felt that things were straightening out again and getting more like they used to be, so it was very disappointing when Aunt came upstairs at bedtime in a flaming temper. I was very glad that both Neil and Donald were asleep when she marched into my room and over to the window, where she stood staring out at the loch.

'Aunt, what is the matter?' I ventured to ask after a moment or two.

'That Somerled!' she burst forth. 'These Macdonalds! Oh, I am a fool to bother about them so much, but I can't help it.'

'What has Somerled done?'

'Nothing except drive that witless young woman about the countryside! When I told him about Mrs. Elton and how she wanted to see him, do you know what he said? He said he had no time to see Mrs. Elton just now. No time! I think he has taken leave of his senses. He does nothing but gaze into that young woman's vapid eyes!'

'Aunt, is Somerled in love with Miss Digby?'

'I suppose you could call it that.' She left the window and came to sit on my bed. 'You may think your aunt is a sour old shrew, Shona, but I do wish that Somerled would stop falling in love, find some well-brought-up girl with some intelligence and marry her. But this Digby girl has neither manners nor intelligence — oh, I suppose she has brains of a sort to have made the success she has, but she is a conceited, ill-behaved, selfish little brat!' I felt an absolute cat, enjoying Aunt being horrible about Dainty Digby.

'Has Somerled been in love before?' I asked.

'A dozen times,' said Aunt, 'but never as inconveniently as this, in the height of the summer season when we have Findlay and Mrs. Elton and Strathdonan and the Camerons from Canada on our hands. Old Mr. Cameron is willing to put up the money to make a good road into the Broad Glen and build a whole ski village, but Somerled is so besotted about that dressmaker's dummy that he has no time to listen.' She broke off, tightened her lips and then said: 'I have no right to call that young woman names. I am sure she is very good at her own job or she would not be where she is. Hers is a very cut-throat profession.'

'Is she really selfish and all those things you said or were you just being angry?' I asked.

'I *was* being angry, but I do find her to be all the things I said. I am angry with myself as much as with Miss Digby, I think. Her kind of singing does not appeal to me much, but it does to millions of people and I always admire people who set out to do a thing and do it well. I was looking forward to meeting the girl, but she has been such a disappointment. She is just a little glutton for flattery and she can be so cruel. She was horrible to Dotty and Coocoo tonight. She despises us all as dowdy frumps and practically says so, but Somerled doesn't seem to notice even. Not that I care a hoot what she thinks of me, but it hurts Dotty and Coocoo, and the fact that Somerled doesn't notice her sneering at them hurts them even more.' Aunt sighed. 'Of course, if it hadn't been this Digby girl it would have been somebody else,' she said. 'Somerled has to have one of these spasms every six months or so, it seems.'

'I thought people fell in love just once and that was that, like in Romeo and Juliet, you know.'

'Romeo and Juliet loved,' said Aunt, 'which is a different thing. It is pretty incurable when people get it the way they did. But this thing Somerled has is a different matter. If only that young woman would overstep the mark sufficiently to wake him up, he will fall out of love and into his senses right away.' Aunt looked thoughtful. 'I should say she is very bad-tempered if things don't go exactly as she wants them to. I wish I knew a bit more about wireless and things—enough to make the microphone or something break down at the right moment at this concert they are arranging.'

'Aunt!' I said, and she laughed.

'Has the date of the concert been fixed yet?' I asked then.

'Next Friday.'

'Aunt, may we stay up for the concert? Neil and Donald and I?'

'I should think so for once if you want to.' She frowned. 'I do wish I could get Somerled to see Mrs. Elton so that we can get on with this thing about Findlay. Every day matters.'

We both stared at the wall for a moment until I said: 'Aunt, I have an idea. If Somerled doesn't see Mrs. Elton before next Friday, invite her and Findlay up for the concert. Neil and Donald and Angus and I will get Somerled to see Mrs. Elton, even if we have to lock the two of them in the dungeons!'

'You are a really bright girl today, Shona,' she said. 'We'll do that.'

One day followed another, but, in spite of what Aunt had said, Somerled showed no sign of falling out of love and I thought it was probably because Dainty Digby was too clever to overstep the mark and wake him up, although Aunt called her vapid and witless because she did not know anything about the Highland Clearances or Celtic stones. I tried hard to think of something I could do to wake Somerled up, but I could not think of anything. Since that night when he drove me back from Strathdonan, when I had told him about Dainty Digby, it had dawned on me that he had been annoyed with me for going about with Fifth Cameron and listening to his guitar, and now, boring as that guitar was, I would have listened to it day and night if I thought it would make Somerled angry and wake him up, but I knew it would not. Somerled was so busy looking at Dainty Digby that he would not notice if I sat around with a hundred Fifths, all of them playing guitars.

Somerled did nothing but drive Dainty Digby around the countryside and none of us knew where they went or what they did, and Neil told Donald that it simply went to show that you could not believe all you read in the newspapers, because all that about Dainty Digby never going anywhere without her mother was a lot of tripe.

'And as for her being a simple homely girl—' I thought, but I did not say it because there was not any point. Neil and Donald would not have understood, but I felt I understood a great deal more since that night Aunt had come into my room in a rage about Somerled.

The result of Somerled not taking any interest in anything except Dainty Digby and forgetting completely that he was a hotel-keeper and the developer of Strathdonan was that the rest of us had to take more interest than ever in the hotel and the development, so that late on the Thursday afternoon before the day of the concert Aunt piled Angus, Neil, Donald and me into the car and we all went rushing over to Strathdonan because the masons had discovered that one of the chimneys had fallen in inside.

It was a pouring wet day, and the dark glen was very grey and dreary with cold little gusts of wind blowing over the black loch and raising angry little flurries of spray. And the wind sighed, too, in the shelter-belt of trees to the north and round the chimney-pots, and the whole house was eerie and horrid. It took Aunt and Angus a long, long time to decide whether the masons should rebuild the chimney or block it up altogether, and while they discussed it all and what it would cost, Neil, Donald and I played at dominoes in the living-room to the left of the front door. Although it was midsummer, we had to have a lamp to see by at half past six, the rain being so heavy and the cloud so low over the glen outside. The electricity was being laid on to the house, but it was not working as yet and, although the oil lamp is beautiful in Angus's lovely house under Ben Vannich, a single oil lamp in this big, square room seemed to do nothing but make moving shadows everywhere. I became more and more bored with the dominoes that Neil had brought and found it more and more difficult to concentrate because I was always looking into the corners where the shadows were. And it was all terribly quiet now, for the joiners and masons had stopped working at six and there were only Aunt and Angus talking quietly away in the back part of the house.

At last, in the middle of a game, I knocked down my row of dominoes and said: 'I'm sick of this. Don't let's play any more. I wish Aunt and Angus would come.'

'I don't like this house very much in the evening time,' Donald said.

'Don't be silly!' Neil said. 'Ghosts and rubbish when it was only Findlay doing a little mischief!'

But he too looked over his shoulder at the shadows in the corner behind him and leaned forward and turned up the wick of the lamp, which only began to smoke so that I had to turn it down again. And, outside, the wind sighed among the trees, squealed across the loch and howled round the chimney-pots.

I was glad when we heard Aunt, Angus and the master mason come through into the hall and the mason say: 'We'll start work on it tomorrow.' Then he must have opened the door, for there was an angry howl of wind before his voice said: 'A dirty night. A blessing we've got the outside walls and roof done. Good night.' We heard the door slam shut and his car drive away as Aunt and Angus came into the room.

'Sorry to have taken so long, you three,' Aunt said. She looked at her watch. 'It isn't seven yet, but in here it might be midnight. This house will be better in winter than in summer, Angus. It is a house for big fires and curtains drawn over these small windows. Goodness, my feet are frozen. Will you all wait till I warm them? We have to let this fire burn down a bit before we can leave it safely, anyhow, now that there are no watchmen on duty.'

The room seemed less eerie and shadowy now, with Aunt sitting at the fire in her stockinged feet and Angus talking to Neil and Donald, but I was quite pleased when Aunt put on her shoes and broke up the last embers of the wood fire. We had all put on our coats, and the three of us and Aunt

were in the hall while Angus was blowing out the lamp when we heard the noise, like a loud yet muffled sob: 'Uh-uh-uh!' We all stood staring at one another and then came a sound like a sad voice calling: 'Oh, there!' it called. 'Oh, there!' It was like the voice of somebody lost, of somebody who called without any hope of being heard. Suddenly, the nearly dark hall seemed to be full of eyes as we all looked at one another and at Angus in the doorway of the room. The noise now came again on a different note, a note urgent and desperate, a combination of the sob and the call: 'Uh there! Uh there! Uh there!' and then it went back to that high, wailing lost note: 'Oh, there! Oh, there!'

'Angus, what can it be?' Aunt whispered.

'Oh, there!' came the voice again.

'Yes!' Aunt called back suddenly. 'We are in the hall! Where are you?'

Stiff with fear, Neil, Donald and I crowded close in round her, and Angus came to her other side as we all looked from the staircase to the kitchen passage and from that to the door that led to the new wing, but no answer came.

'We will help you!' Aunt called. 'Where are you?'

But again there was no answer except the howl of the wind and the noise of the rain outside. Aunt gave a little cough.

'It must have been a trick of the wind, Angus, but it was an uncommonly near-human sort of sound. Shall we get the torch and go over the house?'

'I don't see the point of doing that,' Angus said. 'Whatever it was that made that sound does not want help from us. I think we should leave this place, Elizabeth.'

Goodness, but I was glad to get out of the door into the wind and rain and then into the car, and gladder still when the dark glen of Strathdonan was left behind and we were out in the Broad Glen.

'Aunt,' Neil said then, the first one of us to speak, 'what could it have been? Are there really ghosts?'

'How can one know?' Aunt asked. 'All five of us heard that sound. It might have been the wind in the chimneys like the Ghost Piper at Castle Vannich, but that was a very different sound from the piping at the castle when the wind is west of north.'

'Angus,' said Neil impatiently, appealing to his final authority, 'are there really ghosts?'

'I do not know,' said Angus, which set Neil back on his heels, for he had not believed until then that there could be anything that Angus did not know. 'But,' Angus went on, 'in a house like That One in the Dark Glen where much evil has been done and much misery to others has been caused, I am thinking that some of the evil and misery lives on in it.'

'I don't see what you mean,' said Neil angrily, not that he was angry with Angus, for that could not be, but he was angry with himself because he had been scared and he knew that we all knew it.

'You have been to the Kirk o' Vannich, I think?' Angus asked. 'Did you not find it a fine peaceful old place that made you feel quiet in your spirit? In England there are many such places, but I have been to only two of them — to the Minster at York and to Salisbury Cathedral. It has been said that the stones of such places are steeped in prayer and I am thinking that those bygone prayers bring the feeling of peace and rest to those buildings. Is it not possible, Neil, that bygone evil could bring a feeling of unrest to That House in the Dark Glen?'

'I understand, Angus,' Neil said quietly, 'but that voice calling? It really sounded like a person, didn't it?'

'That part of it I cannot explain,' Angus said. 'It was the wind most likely, but I would argue that in a house with a happier history the wind would make a happier noise. Consider the Ghost Piper of Vannich which we all know is no more than the wind when it blows from a little west of north. The Ghost Piper makes a very poor shape at a tune — the poor fellow has no ear for music at all and he cannot tune his pipes — but he is doing his best to play a tune all the same, the poor misguided creature.'

By the time we had turned into the north drive of the castle, the rain had stopped and we were all feeling much more cheerful and in the pleasant Highland muddle that Angus could get us into with his way of saying one minute that the castle ghost was only the wind and the next minute referring to the ghost in pitying tones as 'a poor misguided creature' as if it were a real person like the police sergeant at Vannich Village.

'And tomorrow evening we have the concert,' he said next. 'I am looking forward to seeing the dancers from Rioch. They are very fine. I used to do a little at the Sword Dance and the Highland Fling myself when I was a little younger, but I am entirely a spectator now.'

'And you will hear Miss Digby sing too,' said Aunt.

'Now that will be very interesting,' Angus commented, 'for Young Kenny tells me that she is what is called a pop singer. I have never heard such a singer before and Young Kenny is not a good explainer. Shona, what sort of singer is a pop singer?'

I could not explain any more than Young Kenny could. It was like when Donald asks: 'What is time?' I feel that

there are pop singers and time and no words for them except
'pop singers' and 'time'.

'A pop singer is a popular singer of popular songs, I think,'
Aunt said.

'But that young lady is not popular with Miss Dorothy
or Miss Constance or myself or, indeed, with your own self,
I am thinking,' said Angus, 'and it is my opinion that her
songs will not be popular with us either. Is there such a
thing as an unpop singer?'

Neil and Donald put their thumbs in their ears, waggled
their fingers and wailed loudly in chorus as Aunt stopped
the car in the courtyard, and as I got out I heard one lady
say to another lady: 'It's all right. It's only Miss Cameron.'
I made a mental note to stop this finger-waggling and wailing act that the boys had. It was only making Aunt seem
more eccentric than she already was.

8. *If You Keep a Thing for Seven Years*

WHEN we came down to breakfast the next morning, there was a pink envelope at Aunt's place with her name typewritten on it and another at Angus's place that said: 'Mr. Angus Mackenzie.' Aunt looked at her envelope as if it might explode and then looked at Angus, who looked back at her and then down at his own envelope.

'Albert,' Aunt said to our waiter, 'where did this come from?' and she pointed at the envelope as if it were a snake.

'Miss Digby's manager gave them to me and a pair for Miss Dotty and Miss Coocoo and one for the Cameron party from Canada. I can recommend the kippers this morning.'

'Miss Digby?' Aunt said, pouncing on the envelope and tearing it open as if she were a savage cannibal disembowelling a missionary before cooking him. 'All right, kippers, Albert,' she said.

Out of the envelope came a pink card which Aunt read before dropping it on the table and saying: 'Well!' When Aunt says this word in the way she said it now, it means anything except what the word 'well' usually means and as she tightened her mouth until she had no lips and stared at the wall, I picked up the card and read it. It said that Miss Dainty Digby requested the pleasure of the company of Miss Cameron and party in the ballroom at eight-thirty that evening. Refreshments. Musical entertainment. 'No admittance without this card.'

Angus had slit his own envelope neatly along the top with his knife, had laid his card on the table and now looked up from it to Aunt.

'I have been living for a fair amount of time now, as you know, Elizabeth,' he said, 'but this is the first time that I have had to carry a piece of pink pasteboard to be allowed into any room in Castle Vannich. No doubt the young lady means well, however.'

'Shall you go, Aunt?' I asked.

Aunt drew in her breath and I was sure she was going to say 'No' in a loud voice, but, suddenly, a queer gleam came into her eyes.

'Yes,' she said, 'I shall go. We shall all go. And Mrs. Elton and Findlay, too.'

'No admittance without this card,' said Donald who had been reading the whole thing aloud.

'We'll take the card with us all right,' said Aunt grimly.

'We don't want to go to any musical entertainment and

refreshments,' Neil protested, 'all dressed up, handing nuts around and feeling dopey!'

'You will do as I say and not be awkward,' said Aunt.

Neil looked like digging his heels in and arguing further, for he does not like parties, but Angus said: 'Now, Neil, do not you be awkward enough to try to stop your aunt being awkward.' He turned to Aunt. 'Elizabeth, why do you want us all to go to this gathering?'

'Simply to be awkward, because we are not really wanted at the gathering,' she said, glaring round at us and attacking her kipper. 'It seems to me that the time for a little awkwardness is ripe and I feel it in my bones that tonight's the night.'

Albert appeared at her elbow. 'Excuse me, but could I have your table as soon as may be? I need it for the men from Aberdeen.'

'*What* men from Aberdeen?' Aunt snapped.

'The men that are fixing up the cameras and stuff in the ballroom for this television do tonight,' Albert explained and hurried away.

'Television cameras in the ballroom!' said Neil. 'Aunt, count me in on this party. Do I wear the kilt or what?'

'Camerons calling and repeating,' said Donald, 'count me in on this party.'

'Yes. Wear the kilt,' said Aunt absently, but then she laughed and said: 'Shona, should I drive down to Jennyville and fetch my hat for this important affair, do you think?'

After lunch, Aunt drove away alone in her car, and I wondered if she really had gone to Jennyville to fetch the hat, but when she came back about six o'clock it was the Ancient Monument which she took out of a box and laid out on her bed. The Ancient Monument is Aunt's one

formal evening dress and Father swears on his honour that
it is even older than the hat, about twice as old, in fact, for
Aunt has had it since at least 1935, he says. It came to be
known as the Ancient Monument because Father said that
Aunt, wearing it, made him think of an ancient monument
that has been preserved by the nation, but whenever it is
mentioned, Mother looks a little wistful and says: 'Liz is
the only woman I know who can wear a dress off and on
for thirty years without having it let out or altered in any
way.' Actually, Aunt dressed in the Ancient Monument looks
rather impressive. It is black and comes down to her feet and
has long, tight sleeves and a high neck, and it has glittery
silver embroidery up to the elbows, round the neck and round
the hem.

'You certainly kept this one for seven years,' I said to
her.

'I keep on hoping that one day I shall get my money's
worth out of it,' she said. 'It was very expensive when I
bought it.' That strange gleam that had been in her eyes
when she decided to go to the party came into them again.
'Maybe it will pay me back tonight. You never know. Go
and change, Shona. I am going down to the village to fetch
Mrs. Elton and Findlay and you and the boys will have to
look after them while I get into that thing.' She pointed
at the Ancient Monument, put on the macintosh with the
leather strap round the middle, and went away.

I had a bath, put on my smartest dress and then went to
find Neil and Donald, who, of course, along with Angus
and Fifth, had made friends with the television men and
were in the ballroom, talking like expert T.V. technicians by
this time. Old Mr. Cameron was in the ballroom, too, but
not being friends with anybody. Instead, he was interfering

with everybody and contradicting everybody. 'You don't want to film this girl singing,' he was saying. 'What you want to film is Jamie the Blacksmith making the gates for my graveyard. What a craftsman! Why do you want to film this girl singing? Say you were to film Jamie, you could have —'

'Father,' said Mrs. Cameron, 'please come and have a rest before the party.'

'I don't want to go to no party. I don't want a rest either. Go away. What do you want with that light over there?' he asked one of the men. 'You don't need a light there. It should be over here.'

'Neil and Donald,' I said, 'come upstairs and change.'

'Aw, Shona,' said Neil, 'we don't want to go to this party now. We've seen all the cameras working and —'

'Upstairs and change,' I said, pointing to the door. I was getting very tough with these brothers of mine in case they grew up to be as difficult as old Mr. Cameron.

'We've been filmed,' said Neil from the bathroom, 'Donald and I. We're in the can. We saw the play-back. We were good, weren't we, Donald?'

'What d'you mean "good"?' I asked.

'We did a shooting act,' Donald said. 'Neil shot at Fifth and me and I died, like this.' He rolled his eyes up, then clutched at his chest and spread-eagled himself on the floor.

'It's in the can?' Neil repeated.

'For posterity,' said Donald, sitting up.

'As if posterity wanted a canful of you and Neil,' I said. 'Get undressed and over into that bath. Hurry up, Neil.'

We were all ready by the time Aunt came back with Mrs. Elton and Findlay, and when Findlay saw me all dressed up in this blue-and-white dress I have and my white kid pumps, he tugged at his grandmother's arm, pointed at me and said: 'Shona! Shona bonnie!'

'Yes, Findlay,' Mrs. Elton said. 'Shona is bonnie, isn't she?' and Findlay came over to me smiling and began to stroke the skirt of my dress gently with his hand. I felt that this was a real compliment, because people like Findlay are not cunning enough to try to flatter you.

Aunt changed in about five minutes and then came into the boys' room, where we all were, looking a little bit like the Great Tower of the castle.

'When Mother goes out in the evening,' Donald said to nobody in particular, 'she wears sort of slippers,' and then we noticed that Aunt's heavy brown brogues were poking their toes out from under her silver-embroidered hem.

'Aunt,' I said, 'look at your feet!'

'My feet? Why?' She looked down. 'Oh, of course,' she said, went away and came back looking more like the Great Tower than ever because of the high heels on her satin slippers.

Angus joined us for dinner and, afterwards, as we went along to the ballroom, I found myself getting more and more excited and I could not think why except that it seemed to have something to do with that queer gleam that had shown in Aunt's eyes. I had never been to a party of this kind before and of course neither had Neil or Donald. Sometimes we have had to hand nuts around, as Neil calls it, at sherry parties at home, but all the parties we had ever been to had been parties among friends, not parties that were publicity stunts, as Aunt said this one was. Neil and Donald were excited again because of the television, and Findlay was excited and a little nervous because of being in a strange place, but, with me, the excitement was of a different kind, as if I were waiting for an explosion or something to happen.

We handed in our cards and passed into the ballroom as if we were going into a theatre or a cinema and, inside, it was not much like a party. Except for Miss Dotty and Miss Coocoo and the Camerons from Canada and us, all the people were strangers and mostly men, and nobody introduced anybody to anybody. Aunt said most of them were journalists who had come to write things about Miss Digby, but one of them came over to us and said to Aunt: 'You are Elizabeth Cameron, the writer, aren't you?' Aunt admitted that she was and I suddenly saw the gleam in her eyes again.

Half of the ballroom floor at the end where the band platform is was covered with chairs for the concert and away beyond the chairs, up on the platform, were Miss Digby, Somerled and the television men. Miss Digby was wearing a long, slim, pink dress with glittery bits on it that sparkled in the lights. Usually I get a thrill out of seeing people in gorgeous clothes, but I was not thrilled by Miss Digby. I was too busy supposing that it was no wonder that Somerled had taken what Aunt called a Macdonald plunge about her.

I could not bear to look at her really, but I simply knew that she looked like all the shiny advertisements for gowns, jewellery, nail varnish, perfume and expensive chocolates that you have ever seen. But in a queer way I suddenly became aware, although I was not looking at her, that she was looking at us where we stood around Aunt, and this made me look right into her face. The first thing she made me think of was a girl who is in my form at school, a girl called Moira Green, who always wants to be first in everything and quite often comes only second or third. Miss Digby looked like Moira Green coming third. I could not understand why, either, because she was so obviously the first person in this

room with everybody staring at her and whispering and I
felt that I was closer to the edge of an explosion than ever.

Then, hurriedly, she came down the steps at the side of
the platform, Somerled following her. They came hurrying
along, Miss Digby looking furious, Somerled striding behind
her with a puzzled face, past the rows of chairs and along
the side of the room towards the door at the end while everybody, including all of us, stared at Miss Digby, wondering
what had gone wrong. She would have gone straight past us,
staring angrily at the floor, but, suddenly, Aunt stepped
forward, stopping her and Somerled, and said in a loud
voice that everybody could hear: 'Good evening, Miss
Digby. How very embarrassing! You and I must go to the
same dressmaker.' And then I noticed that Miss Digby's
dress was exactly the same as the Ancient Monument, only
pink and, being pink and Miss Digby being much shorter
than Aunt, it did not look at all monumental. In fact, standing close to Aunt while everybody stared, Miss Digby looked
rather insignificant and a bit silly, I thought, and, although
I did not like her, I felt sorry for her because she was in such
a rage that she could not think of anything to say.

I think we might all have stood there for ever — all of
us, except Aunt — frozen with embarrassment, if it had not
been for Findlay, who, as he had done upstairs with my
dress, went over to Miss Digby, stroked her long, pink
dress with his hand, looked up at her smiling and said:
'Bonnie, bonnie.' Miss Digby looked at Findlay, drew back,
shuddered and said in a voice that was almost a scream:
'He's an idiot! Don't touch me! Go away! Go away!' and
she jerked her arm, throwing Findlay's hand off and frightening him so that he backed in between Mrs. Elton and
Aunt, his eyes wide and staring.

My brother Neil, especially when on parade at a grown-up affair like this, is quite well-behaved, but he has a violent red-haired temper, which now blazed up and he sprang towards Miss Digby and shouted: 'How dare you do that to Findlay! You're ghastly, beastly and absolutely bloody!' And then Donald stamped forward, stared up through his glasses and said: 'Camerons calling and repeating: You're ghastly, beastly and absolutely bloody!'

At first I felt stunned. I had never heard Neil and Donald use the word 'bloody' before. And it all happened in about two seconds, and you know the number of things you can think of in two seconds, once you get over feeling stunned. Gosh, I thought, there is going to be one unholy row about this, but all the same she *was* horrible to Findlay, and Neil is quite right, although this is probably the end of our visits to Castle Vannich, but I don't care because Neil is my brother and the first time Father put us on the train by ourselves to come to Aunt's he said we were to stick together whatever happened because a lost child is only a lost child, but three children together on their own are a body of opinion and so the three of us are going to stick together now and be a body of opinion, I thought, so I stepped forward beside Neil and Donald and said: 'We are leaving now, Miss Digby, with our friend Findlay. Good night.'

And then I realised how dreadful all this was, with every-body staring and Aunt standing there like the Great Tower. I wished the floor would open and swallow us, that we need never have to face Aunt when we got upstairs, but suddenly, with one arm round Findlay's shoulders, she put her other hand on my shoulder and said: 'Good night, Miss Digby. Come, Mrs. Elton. Come, children.' As we moved away, I heard Miss Dotty and Miss Coocoo say good night, too, and then the Camerons from Canada. At the door of the ball-room, Aunt stopped and we all looked back. Angus, very old and dignified, was walking slowly across the floor towards Miss Digby and Somerled, and there was dead silence as he said in his polite, quiet voice: 'I will say good night, too, Miss Digby.' Then he squared his shoulders, looked up at Somerled and said: 'Macdonald, I will bid you good — '

But Somerled interrupted him. 'It is too early to wish me good night, Angus,' he said. 'I think you and I will go for a walk. Good night, Miss Digby,' and the two of them came towards us, leaving the girl alone in the middle of the floor in the pink dress with all the lights shining on her and the huge cameras looming up behind like the skeletons of prehistoric monsters in a museum.

When we came along to the hall, Findlay was still trembling and he looked up at his grandmother and said: 'Findlay go to bed.'

'Yes, Findlay,' Aunt said, 'we'll take you home to bed. Shona, run up for our three coats and I'll take Findlay home right away.'

Neil and Donald came with me and, as I grabbed the coats, I said: 'You two stay here. I'll be right back.' I ran down with the coats and as I watched the car drive away I saw Somerled and Angus going out of the Great Yett with their walking-sticks, going for an evening walk as they used to do before Miss Digby came.

When I went back up to the boys' room, they were sitting side by side on the edge of Neil's bed, looking very guilty and rather comic, all dressed up in the kilt and their best white shirts and all clean, with their hair neatly brushed. As a rule, when Neil and Donald have done something that makes them look guilty, they also look very grubby.

'Cheer up,' I said. 'I believe this is going to be all right.'

'Are you dotty?' said Neil, ripping off his tartan tie. 'Listen, Shona, can you remember what I *said*?'

'I told you already what we said,' said Donald. 'We said she was ghastly and beastly and absolutely bloody, didn't we, Shona?'

'Yes, and she is and she was, even the bloody bit.'

'But I said it first, didn't I?' Neil asked.

'Listen, Muggins, when it comes to temper in this family, *you* always get in first. Donald and I are used to it.'

'Where's Aunt?' he said, looking uneasily about the room. Then he blinked. 'Oh, of course, taking Findlay home.'

'Neil, stop worrying. I feel it in my bones that this is going to be all right.'

'You and your bones! We should never have gone to that bloody party.'

'Neil Cameron, stop saying that word.'

'Camerons calling and repeating: that bloody party!'

'Donald, stop saying that silly rigmarole and don't use that word!'

'The trouble with our family is,' said Neil, 'they go on and on about good manners and then get you in spots where you *can't* have any manners. That stinking Digby dame—'

'Look,' I interrupted him, 'the best thing you two can do is get to bed and pretend to be asleep when Aunt gets back. I don't think there is going to be any trouble about this carry-on, but if she comes in here and finds you "stink-ing-ing" and "bloody-ing" there will be more than trouble.'

'That makes sense,' said Neil, 'and she will calm down by morning. Donald, get undressed and get into bed.'

Donald was so astounded at Neil taking charge like this

that he was undressed and in bed in two minutes flat, and before Aunt got back they were both really asleep, for she was gone a long time, helping to calm Findlay down, and Neil's blind fits of temper always make him tired.

I had meant to get myself a new book from the library in the Great Tower that day, but had forgotten, so I went to Aunt's room where, I knew, there would be bound to be something to read. When I went to the table that is always piled with books, I found something that was very unusual to find in Aunt's room, one of the women's glossy magazines, inside the tartan hotel cover, which lie about on the tables in the drawing-room. It was called *Woman With It* and was full of the usual shiny coloured pictures of models wearing everything from corsets to fur coats and in the centre pages there was a big headline: 'Top Taste' and pictures of Dainty Digby, a princess, an American woman ambassador, and a French actress, and underneath: 'Their latest choice for the evening.' When I turned the page to see what they had chosen, there was a coloured picture of a model wearing the pink version of the Ancient Monument and, alongside it, the words: 'An echo of the sophistication of the '30's, chosen by Dainty Digby,' and alongside *this*, in the margin, there was a long thoughtful squiggle made with Aunt's red pen, the sort of squiggle she makes when she reads something that gives her an idea. Her books are full of such squiggles and I could imagine her making this one while that queer gleam came into her eyes.

By the time she came back, I was undressed and in bed, but I was certain now that there was not going to be any trouble about how we had behaved at the party. I heard her go to her own room, and made up my mind that if she did not come in to see me, I would go to see *her*. I had deliberately left that magazine, open at the Dainty Digby dress page, lying on her pillow. She tapped at my door and came in, the old macintosh hanging open over the Ancient Monument, a funny smile on her face as if she were the one who had told her hostess at the party that she was bloody.

'How is Findlay?' I asked.

'Quite calm again. How is our Neil?'

'Quite calm again, too,' I said, 'and asleep. Aunt, Neil didn't mean to be rude, but he simply can't help blowing up like that when—'

'I think you all behaved absolutely beautifully,' she interrupted me. 'It was appalling, really, if you see what I mean, and I don't think we should mention it to your parents; but at the same time it was absolutely splendid. I haven't behaved so outrageously for years, but, goodness, I did enjoy myself,' she said, and giggled as if she were in the second form.

'Aunt, you wore the Ancient Monument on purpose?'

She put one foot forward and looked down at the embroidered hem.

'Yes,' she said, not looking at me.

'But how did you know that Miss Digby would wear the pink?'

'I didn't. I took a gamble on that. But I sort the guests' mail, you know and the box with the Fontanelle label arrived only yesterday. I had a feeling that tonight would be the night and it was.'

'It was luck that you happened to see that magazine,' I said, feeling like a conspirator.

Aunt looked up at me indignantly. 'There was no luck about it,' she said sternly. 'I saw that magazine because I try to be a good hotel-keeper. Miss Digby is obviously glossy-

magazine-fodder, and before she came to stay I studied them
all assiduously,' she told me virtuously, but she spoiled her
goody-goody hotel-keeper act by adding: 'I think she will
go away tomorrow. I hope she does. Well, it is time you went
to sleep, Shona. I saw Somerled on my way upstairs. He,
Angus and I are going down to see Mrs. Elton tomorrow
and I'd like you to come too, to keep Mrs. Elton up to the
mark. You seem to be able to handle her much better than
I can.'

'Never mind,' I said in a patronising voice that made her
laugh, 'you handled Dainty Digby terribly well. Goodness,
what a temper she was in! But she looked rather sad when
we all came away and left her all alone in the middle of
the floor with all those lights and cameras around.'

'She will get over it,' Aunt said. 'And I don't think all
our bad behaviour was really necessary, after all. I gather
that Somerled was finding out that she loves cameras and
bright lights more than she loved him, anyway. Our little
débâcle only brought him to his senses a little more quickly,
and besides, I found it highly enjoyable. I don't care what
any of you three grow up into, but don't get swelled heads,
will you? I couldn't bear it.'

I suddenly remembered about Neil and Donald being so
cock-a-hoop about getting themselves filmed, and as she went
to the door, I said: 'Talking about swelled heads, Donald
and Neil got themselves filmed today when the men were
testing the cameras and Donald told me quite solemnly that
he and Neil were in the can for posterity.'

Aunt laughed. 'Poor posterity!' she said and then she
became solemn as she repeated: 'Yes, poor posterity! Good
night, Shona,' she added and went away.

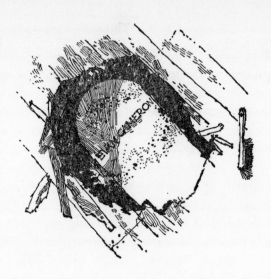

9. *The Lost Voice Found*

WHEN we came down the next morning, although it was only a little after eight, Somerled and Angus had already gone away to Strathdonan, leaving a message that they would meet Aunt at Mrs. Elton's at eleven in the forenoon. After breakfast, Neil and Donald went across the courtyard to watch Jamie the Blacksmith and his son working on the graveyard gates and I went with Aunt to her office to help her sort the mail.

'Somerled is back on his form, thank goodness,' she said. 'Take this bundle of letters through to Albert in the dining-room, Shona.' When I came back to the office I said: 'The Digby party is leaving, Aunt. The luggage is being put into the car.'

'I thought as much. Good. Better empty rooms than bad tenants, as Angus says, although to call the Digby party bad is very unfair. They are bad only in relation to us eccentrics here. Run along to the reception office and say that I am reminding them about those people in Edinburgh who were interested in any sudden cancellation of bookings.'

When I came out of the reception office, Dainty Digby was standing in the hall glaring at a newspaper, and when she saw me, she threw it angrily down on a chair and went out and got into the car, so I picked up the paper and looked at the front page. As if there were some mysterious connection between newspapers and my brother Donald, he appeared at my elbow like a genie out of a bottle and Neil appeared at my other side as Donald read aloud: '"Happy occasion at Castle Vannich."'

'Gosh,' said Neil 'it's *us*! That's me saying "bloody" to that dame last night. *Father* gets this paper. He'll see it!'

'"Dainty Digby,"' Donald read in his dreamy reading voice from under the photograph, '"chatting to Miss Elizabeth Cameron, noted Highland writer, at Castle Vannich last night. Full report on Page Six."' We all sat down on the floor and hustled over to page six, but the full report did not mention Neil, Donald or me. It merely said a lot of stuff about how successful the concert was and what a pleasant time everybody had.

'Well,' said Neil indignantly, 'of all the tripy nonsense!'

'Look, Muggins,' I said, 'it is just as well the paper doesn't tell what really happened,' and we turned back to the picture again. 'The picture looks all right. You would never know what is going on. And it's a good picture of Aunt, isn't it?'

'I think it's a shame,' Donald said sadly. 'They probably won't use the picture of Aunt in her hat any more now they've got this one. It's a shame. That hat was the very first thing I ever read in a newspaper!'

K

Quite soon, Aunt and I had to leave to be at Mrs. Elton's by eleven o'clock. Aunt was very thoughtful and quiet at first as she drove along, and then she said: 'I have to admit that Somerled seems to have the Midas touch. There were three enquiries about ski-ing holidays at Strathdonan in the mail this morning. We haven't advertised it as yet, but the news is getting around.'

'That's marvellous.'

'It would be marvellous if the beastly place looked anything like being ready in time,' Aunt said. 'Drat Somerled and his crazy plunges. We have lost a good three weeks on this Digby nonsense. It's odd,' she went, talking more to herself than to me. 'The clan system is supposed to be as dead in the Highlands as the feudal system is in England, but the clan system is not dead here at Vannich. All these masons and joiners get through twice as much work when Somerled is there with them. Angus and I are no substitute for him.'

'But Somerled larks about most of the time, Aunt. And he makes the young boys lark about, too. The master joiner said that the young boys were always missing because Somerled was showing them how to cast flies over the loch.'

'I know, but the curious, paradoxical fact remains that more work gets done when Somerled is apparently wasting the time of half the workers. Well, here we are. And Somerled and Angus are here already. He is definitely back on the job.'

When we went into the house, Mrs. Elton was sitting by the fire crying, with Angus trying to comfort her while Somerled stood in the middle of the floor, looking very large, awkward and helpless.

'Shona,' said Aunt, 'go and make a cup of tea. Somerled,

go with her and give her a hand. Now, Mrs. Elton, what has gone wrong? Where is Findlay?'

'Findlay is down on the beach feeding the swans,' said Angus, 'and there is nothing that is wrong. Mrs. Elton is in a misery of tears because she is happy at having told her whole dreadful story at last, and if you will kindly go to the scullery, Elizabeth, taking the others with you and stop behaving like the police sergeant, the poor misguided man; we will be all right very soon.'

Somerled winked at me because of Aunt getting a ticking-off from Angus and the three of us went through to the scullery.

As I put the kettle on, Aunt took up a commanding position in the middle of the floor, looked sternly at Somerled and said:

'Well, have you got the name of this wretched man out of her? I can't wait to get started on this claim. Never mind Shona's being here. She has done more good in this horrid business than any of us. Speak up. What was his name?

Where did he live?' Aunt did sound a little like a policeman, firing these questions at Somerled, but she was like this, I knew, because she was so anxious to help Findlay. Aunt often sounds angry and abrupt when she is at her most kind. Somerled stood looking down at us both for a moment before he said very quietly: 'The man's name, Liz, was Hugh Gordon and he lived at a place called Strathdonan.'

'What!' Aunt's face seemed to fall apart with astonishment, and she sat down 'Bonk!' on the one scullery chair as if her knees had given way. After a moment she said: 'Tell us, Somerled. Start at the beginning and tell us everything.'

Somerled pushed his fingers through his hair, looking sadly away out of the window towards the Firth, where we could see Findlay, a tiny figure, far along the beach, feeding the swans.

'There isn't much to tell,' he said. 'Mary, Mrs. Elton's daughter — her only child, by the way — was a hospital nurse and very pretty. You will see photographs of her later. She met Gordon in London, they fell in love and there it was. They were married' — he jerked his head towards the door of the living-room — 'Mrs. Elton has the marriage certificate and Findlay's birth certificate and everything. I gather the marriage went wrong right from the start — Gordon was already a drunkard, of course, but the girl didn't know that. Then Findlay was born and discovered to be a little backward, and Gordon took a hate at him. When Findlay was nine, Mary brought the boy to her mother, but she herself went back to Gordon. She stuck to Gordon all the way through, Heaven knows why.' Somerled paused, frowning. 'It is queer how people can go on being attached and attracted to people even when there are things about them that they loathe rather.' He looked straight at Aunt, then at me and then back at Aunt, and I knew he was trying to make us understand that there were things he 'loathed rather' about Dainty Digby, although he went on spending all his time with her.

'Yes, Somerled,' Aunt said, 'that can happen.'

'Then Gordon and Mary came up to Strathdonan. He couldn't afford to live in London any longer. But Mrs. Elton kept hoping that one day Mary would leave him and she wanted to be near her daughter. Then old Mrs. Graham, who used to live in this cottage, died and Mrs. Elton wrote to me, saying that she was a native of the county, telling me about her orphan grandson, as she called him, who was mentally retarded and saying she had heard from a friend about this empty cottage and how she hadn't much money but wanted Findlay to live in the country instead of in London and so—'

'You wrote back saying to come to the cottage, but she needn't pay any rent for it,' said Aunt.

'I did nothing of the sort!'

'You did. I saw the copy of the letter.'

'I didn't write it. Miss Miller in the office wrote it.'

'Shona,' Aunt said, 'remind me to tell Miss Miller that I would like to have Castle Vannich for the winter, but I can't afford to pay any rent. I'm sure she'll let me have it. Miss Miller is terribly kind-hearted.'

'Oh, shut up, Liz!' said Somerled. 'Anyhow, Mrs. Elton and Findlay came here. She told me that one day she took Findlay up to Strathdonan, but Gordon chased them from the door with a stick. She never went again and she never saw her daughter again either after that day, when she and Findlay saw her looking out through the window. The girl was a prisoner, really.' He shivered and shook his head as if he were trying to shake the thought of Mrs. Elton's daughter out of his mind and then he said: 'Mrs. Elton is terribly muddle-headed, Liz. When the tragedy — when Gordon and Mary died, she got a frightful shock, but it was my leaping in and buying Strathdonan that stopped her making a claim against Gordon's estate. She thought in her muddled fashion that it would harm *me* in some way, and she didn't want to do that. But Angus and I have made her see that whatever is left of what I paid for Strathdonan naturally belongs to Findlay. Gordon hasn't left any will or anything.'

'But will there be anything left when his debts are paid?' Aunt asked. 'Not much, I should think, but it doesn't matter. Findlay will be all right as long as the rest of us are around.' Somerled grinned. 'If Strathdonan pays off, we'll be up to our ears in money.'

Aunt shook her head and smiled. 'Somerled the Gambler the Second,' she said, 'fair ladies and all. Oh, well.'

Angus poked his head in at the door. 'I do not think I have ever known three people take longer to make a drop of tea,' he said.

'It's ready, Angus,' I told him. 'We were waiting for you to ask us to come.'

'Come, Shona,' said Mrs. Elton. 'Macdonald, it was Shona and her brothers who made me make up my mind to speak to you about Findlay.'

'Shona and her brothers are quite good at making people make up their minds,' Somerled said, and I felt myself blushing, for I knew he was remembering how awful we had been to Dainty Digby the evening before.

'But you are not to worry any more about Findlay or

about anything, Mrs. Elton,' he went on. 'There is a new school for people like Findlay being built at Rioch and he could go there and come home for the weekends. Miss Cameron will find out all about it.'

She was very trembly and shaky and wiped her blue eyes again as Aunt handed her a cup of tea. 'You are being very good to my boy and me,' she said, 'and you will never regret it. He is a good boy with nothing of his wicked father in him.'

'Except one thing,' said the quiet voice of Angus, 'a thing that can be used for goodness or badness. That boy is a born gamekeeper or poacher or shepherd, Mrs. Elton. Poaching is a little out of fashion these days, but Vannich still needs men that can walk quietly and with knowledge about the hills and glens, using their eyes and their ears. Findlay does not need to go to any school. We must teach him not to be afraid of Kenny the Shepherd any more and then he can go along with Young Kenny and learn about the sheep and stay here with his granny and not at a strange school in Rioch, in the town, where no man in his senses wants to live.'

'Findlay is hardly afraid of Kenny the Shepherd at all now,' I said, 'because Kenny had been giving him rides in the old Land-Rover. In fact, the only person Findlay is really afraid of now is old Mr. Cameron, because of his stick, and Mr. Cameron can't walk without it, so it is rather difficult. But we must think of something.'

We talked on about Findlay for a little longer until Somerled got up and said: 'Look here, you lot, it's past lunchtime and I want to get back to Strathdonan this afternoon to start tearing up the floor in that old drawing-room.' We all got up.

'Now don't worry any more, Mrs. Elton. And I'll send the slater down to see to that roof for you. You should have reported it to the office long ago.'

We all went back to the castle for lunch, which Somerled had with Angus, Aunt and all of us, which was just like things used to be before what Aunt was calling the Digby Débâcle and, over the coffee, Somerled said to Aunt: 'If you've got nobody's ancestors to look up in your office this afternoon, Liz, why don't you and those three come over to the Strath? You might as well know the worst. I think there is water rising under the foundations of that drawing-room.'

'Great Heaven!' said Aunt.

'I tore up a couple of boards this morning and there are more boards underneath, but they are rotten and soaking wet, like sponges.' He grinned mischievously. 'Rising water would account for that sobbing ghost you and Angus heard, too,' he said. 'After all, what is a sob but water rising? Only this isn't a ghost in tears, it's Loch Donan leaking along some underground channel or something.'

'Go on, smarty-pants,' Aunt told him, 'laugh your red head off at a superstitious old Highland haybag, but I still don't trust that house.'

'No, nor I,' said Angus quietly.

As soon as lunch was over, we all set off for Strathdonan, but it was nearly three o'clock before we arrived there because we had been late for lunch in the first place. Somerled went jumping up the steps and threw open the door of the drawing-room to see how far the men had got with the work, and then stood back nonplussed because nothing at all had been done. The only part of the floor that had been lifted was the little bit he himself had torn up that morning.

As we stood there, the master joiner, a man of about sixty, came down the stairs.

'Dash it, Gallie,' Somerled said, 'I expected to see that floor up by now.'

'When yourself was not here, Macdonald, we thought we would just finish off the work above stairs first.'

'I see,' said Somerled as Aunt drew me by the sleeve of my sweater into the living-room across the hall. 'It's just on three o'clock,' Somerled went on. 'Knock off for half an hour for a cup of tea, Gallie, and we'll have a go at that floor afterwards.'

'Very good, Macdonald,' the man said, and he went away while Somerled, Angus, Neil and Donald went upstairs.

'Shall I get you a cup of tea from the men's pot?' I asked Aunt.

'Yes, please.' She smiled. 'Gallie and his joiners were not going to tackle that room on their own. That's what I meant by the clan system here at Vannich. They will *follow* Somerled into it and do what he asks them to do, but they would not tackle it on their own. It is as if they were still following the blue banner with the White Hind of Vannich on it. Thank you, Shona. You had better bring cups for Somerled and Angus too.'

As I went through the passage to the kitchen, I could hear all the workmen in there talking in low voices, but when I went in they stopped at once and then began to speak again in quite different voices, teasing me about Fifth Cameron being my boy-friend and asking if I would invite them to my wedding, but I felt that, before I came into the kitchen, they had been talking about that horrid drawing-room.

I carried the cups of tea through on the tin tray and called upstairs to Somerled and Angus, who came down to the living-room, but Neil and Donald went outside, where Young Kenny was rattling about with his tractor, hauling away trailer-loads of brushwood and piling them up down on the shore of the loch to make a bonfire.

'The men don't like that room,' Somerled said as he took his cup, 'but it has got to be done.'

'They will do it, Macdonald,' Angus said.

'Yes. We'll all do it,' Aunt said.

Everybody spoke so quietly and as if they did not want some unknown 'thing' to hear them that I felt quite shivery and, to make things worse, the sun disappeared, as it was always doing, behind the hills and clouds of Strathdonan and the room grew dim. And then the noise came. First the sob: 'Uh-uh-uh!' and then the lost voice calling: 'Oh, there! Oh, there!' and then 'Uh-uh-uh!' again and the urgent: 'Uh there! Uther Uther!'

'What the devil is that?' Somerled whispered, his whole body stiffening.

'They tell me,' Aunt whispered cruelly, 'it is nothing but water rising under the floor.'

'Oh, there! Oh, there!' called the voice again, high above the rattle of Kenny's tractor outside, and I felt my spine crawling as the door of the room opened. But it was only Mr. Gallie with all his other joiners and apprentices behind him, not making a sound, their eyes wide and staring. Somerled held up his hand and whispered: 'Have you heard this before?'

'No, Macdonald.'

'But I have heard it before,' Angus said in a voice like a breath of summer wind, 'and I know now what it is. It is Findlay calling for his mother, poor boy.' .

'Oh, there! Oh, there!' came the voice.

'Findlay cannot sound the letter M,' Aunt whispered.
'You are right, Angus.'

'He is in the room over there,' Angus said. 'Keep quiet,
everybody. We will put Shona in, for he is fond of Shona.'
He looked down at me. 'You will go, Shona?' I nodded.
'Just walk in as if nothing was wrong and speak to him as
you usually do.'

My knees wobbled as the knot of men made a way for
Angus and me to cross the hall to the door of that room,
even although I was certain now that it was only Findlay
inside. As Angus put his hand on the door handle, there was
a loud rattle from Young Kenny's tractor outside and it gave
me an idea of something to say to Findlay, so, when the door
opened, I walked through and said:

'Hello, Findlay. Come for a ride on the —' and then I
stopped, for Findlay was sitting on the edge of an enormous
hole in the floor. He had about a quarter of the floor of the
room torn up.

When he first turned his head to look at me, it was as if
he did not know me. People like Findlay and my brother
Iain live in two worlds, you see. Iain lives part of the time
in what Aunt and I call his 'world of over the hills and far
away,' which is a happy place for him; but, while he is in it,
he does not remember about having a father, mother, sister
and brothers because he does not need us in that lovely land
among his dreams. Now I saw that Findlay also had two
worlds, but that Findlay's far-away one was not a happy
place like Iain's — it was a horrid place where he searched
for his lost mother and where people might chase him with
sticks and be cruel to him. And he was glad to come out of
that world.

'Shona!' he said, smiling at me as he sat on the floor at

the edge of the hole he had made. 'Shona!' and then he looked down at the hole, turned a sad, worried face to me, and said very low: 'Shona, Findlay bad,' and he pointed to the broken-up mess of wood all round him, shaking his head sadly, not remembering that it was being in that horrible lost world that had made him destructive like this.

'No!' I said loudly. 'Findlay is *not* bad. You are a *good* boy, Findlay, helping the Macdonald to take up the floor!'

''acdonald?' he said smiling. 'Findlay good?'

Somerled came through the doorway. 'Hi there, Findlay,' he said.

'By gosh, you *have* been getting on with the work, good chap!' Findlay looked pleased and now pointed at the hole with pride and tore up another piece of rotten wood.

'That's the stuff!' said Somerled, and ripped up another piece.

Angus now opened the door wide and he and Aunt came into the room while all the joiners began to laugh at Findlay and Somerled ripping and tearing away, and Findlay became quite uproarious with pleasure, jumped into the hole and began sloshing out handfuls of wet spongy wood from the next layer.

The joiners fetched their tools and one of the boys brought a wheelbarrow and began to collect the debris that Somerled and Findlay were throwing about and, there being no show without Punch, Neil and Donald arrived and joined in the ripping and tearing-up. Donald, who likes the dirtiest places best, got into the hole with Findlay and now Aunt provided them with a short fire shovel each and they dug the rotten, wet wood out and threw it into the wheelbarrow. The smell was abominable, like the worst of bad drains, but the more appalling the smell became, the happier Findlay and Donald seemed to be.

'Take off the top boards,' Aunt said to the joiners, 'and leave what is underneath to the boys. They like it and what people like won't make them ill, but I feel the rest of us might get diphtheria.' She was turning away when Donald said: 'Hi, chaps, there's writing in this hole.' He scraped with his shovel on stone. 'Camerons calling and repeating: Writing in this hole.' He scraped again. 'Gosh, it says "eron".' Another scrape. 'It says "Cameron". Aunt, our name is written on a stone in here!'

'What?' Aunt looked at Angus, who looked back at her, and there was dead silence all around as the two of them, their handkerchiefs over their noses, stepped forward to the edge of the hole. Aunt looked down and said: 'A brush, somebody. Is there a scrubbing-brush?'

One of the apprentices ran away and came back with two old scrubbing-brushes and she gave one each to Donald and Findlay.

'Carefully, Donald,' she said. 'Findlay will imitate what you do. Brush the part to the left of the word "Cameron".'

We all gathered round, Somerled shining his torch down, as the two brushes began to push away the wet stuff like smelly sawdust, and it was like magic to see the letters n, a, v and a capital E appear, spelling the name 'Evan' backwards. Aunt looked up at Angus and Somerled, and her eyes were full of tears. 'Camerons were calling in this house all right,' she said. 'That looks to me like the gravestone of Evan Cameron the Third's ancestors.'

The two boys had gone on brushing, and Donald now said: 'Aunt, there's another stone just next to this one!'

'Here,' said Neil, 'let me get down into that hole!'

And now all of us forgot all about the smell of stagnant water and rotten wood. Soon the joiners had torn off the first floor and we were all scraping and brushing at the spongy stuff underneath, and there would come shouts of: 'Mackenzie!' and 'Gallie!' and 'Sinclair!' as gravestone after gravestone was uncovered. At last, Somerled stood up and shouted: 'Time up, men! It's nearly seven o'clock.'

'Ach, Macdonald,' said an apprentice called Davie disgustedly, 'we haven't come on *my* people's stone yet!'

'Now, then, Davie Farquhar,' said Angus, 'that will be enough of your impatience. If the Macdonald says it is time, it is time. It is likely that there is another layer of stones beneath this one, for it is my opinion that all the stones from the old graveyard in the glen are in here and the Farquhar stone, I have no doubt, will be at the very bottom, the way you were always at the bottom of the class at school.'

Everybody laughed, including the impatient Davie, but not Somerled. 'What sort of men were they that buried their family gravestones in this hole?' he asked disgustedly, and a queer silence fell, for all of us round about were aware that the stones must have been taken from the graveyard and brought here by our own ancestors.

'I will tell you what sort of men they were, Macdonald,' said Angus quietly into the silence. 'They were men like all of us here with the exception of yourself.' Somerled was standing a little apart and his kilt, open-necked white shirt and silver-mounted sgian in the top of his stocking suddenly made him look very different from all the other men in overalls and the boys in their blue jeans. He turned his head and looked at Angus.

'You are the first Macdonald to obey the orders of another man and that only since you became a hotel-keeper, and there are some who would say that you are not very good at taking orders even yet, although I will grant that you do your best. The men who took these stones from their rightful place and brought them here were the forefathers of us who are here now,' Angus said, looking round at us all and back to Somerled, 'but they had the misfortune to be dependent for their living on a bad man.'

'Bad 'an,' said Findlay, still brushing gently at one of the stones.

'If a man has a wife and children, Macdonald,' Angus went on, 'and a bad master, he carries out his master's orders and asks God to forgive him. And God forgives the man, but, in the end, the Devil gets the master, I am thinking.'

We were all quiet and this room was not horrible any longer. The gravestones lay, seeming to look up at us with the confidence that we would restore them to the place where they belonged.

'Come, Findlay,' Angus said gently, 'put down your brush now. You are the cleverest boy in the whole of Glen Vannich this day.'

Findlay climbed out of the hole and then his eyes changed, darkening and growing wide, and he said: ''other?'' on a high, questioning note.

'Mother has gone to bed, Findlay,' Aunt told him and he looked pleased. 'Come along out to the car now.'

'Car,' said Findlay, and ran outside.

10. *The Treasure of Strathdonan*

As we drove back to the castle we were all very excited, talking about our discovery, but, as we were turning into the north drive, Aunt said to Neil, Donald and me: 'Now, not another word about Strathdonan except in our own rooms upstairs. And that goes for you as well, Somerled and Angus. The news won't be at the castle as yet, not among the guests at least, and if old Mr. Cameron hears about that gravestone tonight, he'll be off to Strathdonan in his pyjamas.'

'Liz is right, Angus,' Somerled said.

'As soon as we get in,' Aunt said, 'I'll see Mrs. Cameron and tell her about the gravestones, and she and Mr. Fourth will know the best time to tell the old man. That old heart of his is not to be played with.'

'All right, Liz,' Somerled agreed. 'Shona, Neil,

Donald and I will be as quiet as a bunch of clams.'

This had the effect of making Neil and Donald look as if they would burst with importance and untold secrets all through dinner, and if I had not known about Strathdonan already, I would have known at once that they were hiding something, but the hotel guests, of course, did not know my brothers as well as I did and did not suspect anything.

After dinner, all of us and Mr. and Mrs. Fourth went to Aunt's office, and Mrs. Fourth said. 'I have had an idea. Let's send Shona in to tell Father the news. He won't raise the roof with Shona as he might with you or me, Evan.'

Everybody seemed to think this was a good idea. Quite often, I went to visit old Mr. Cameron in his sitting-room in the evenings since I stopped being his personal maid, but now, as I tapped at the door while the others stood in the passage and he called me to come in, I felt I had spent the whole day being pushed through doors and really was turning into Shona the Spearhead, as Somerled was whispering.

When I went in, Mr. Cameron laid aside the book he was reading, and said: 'That aunt of yours certainly knows her stuff about these Highlands here. Well, what you been doing all day?'

'I have been over at Strathdonan all afternoon.'

'How's it coming?'

'It's getting on. Somerled and the men started work on that smelly old drawing-room today,' I said.

'So he's attending to business again instead of chasing that little petticoat with the store-boughten eyelashes?' he said in his sharp, creaky voice, and I could imagine Somerled's embarrassment where they were all listening outside. 'You tell that fellah to come and see me when he has a spare minute. Where is he right now?'

'He is with Aunt, but I'll tell him to come to you as soon as he is free.'

'You do that, girlie. If he'll listen to me, that Strathdonan development could be quite a project.'

'That smelly old drawing-room had two floors in it,' I said, trying to get back to the business in my head and away from the business in old Mr. Cameron's head, which, if you had known him, you would recognise as being quite difficult.

'We could start with ten chalets on that wooded place behind the church,' he said.

'Both the floors were rotten and we tore them up,' I said.

'And later on we could put another dozen on that slope towards Jennyville.'

'And when we tore the floors up, what do you think was *underneath*?' I said very loudly.

'Underneath what?'

'The floors.'

'What floors?'

'In the drawing-room at Strathdonan.'

'A swamp for my money,' he said, 'going by the smell.'

'You've lost your money,' I said.

He now really was paying attention. 'Now, you listen to me,' he said, glaring at me sternly, 'I been in the building trade for over fifty years and I haven't lost any money in it yet. There is water under that floor!' and he went 'bonk!' on the carpet with his stick.

'Oh, yes, there's water,' I said, 'but there's something else, too.'

'What?'

'Stones.'

'What d'ye mean — stones?'

'Gravestones,' I said and I put both my hands on top of

his hand that held the stick upright beside his chair. 'Mr. Cameron, all the gravestones from your graveyard are in there. No! Please stay still. I'll tell you all about it.'

'Tell me then, girlie.'

'The very first one we found has three Evan Camerons on it and Aunt says it belongs to your people.'

He looked up at me and his old eyes looked queer.

'Shona, you wouldn't be making up a story to amuse an old man? Because, see, it isn't amusing.'

'I'm not making it up. If you will sit still and try not to get too excited, I'll get Aunt and Angus and Somerled.'

'I'll sit right here, Shona, honest to God,' he said.

When I went out to the hall, Mr. Fourth told me that I had done a fine job and I felt better, for old Mr. Cameron had suddenly become so humble and quiet and unlike himself that I had felt scared. Then we all went into the room again.

'Is this true about all these gravestones under that floor?' Mr. Cameron asked.

'Yes, sir,' Somerled said.

'And one with —,' his voice shook, '— three Evan Camerons on it?'

'Yes,' Aunt said, 'and the first one is described as the son of Evan Cameron, so you have been masquerading all your life. You are not the Third at all — you are at least the Seventh and more likely the seventy-seventh.'

'I can hardly believe it!' He reached out his hand to Fifth. 'Hi, son, is this not the best vacation you ever had?'

'I'll say!' said Fifth.

And then old Mr. Cameron noticed the little phial of pills that Mrs. Fourth was holding and because he was so much in the habit of having to be cross about something, he said: 'Put those goddam pills away, Louise! I don't need pills. I just got me a bunch of ancestors.' He then pointed the stick at Somerled. 'Here you, these stones got to be put back in my graveyard where they belong!'

'Yourself had better come over there in the morning and see to taking them out of our road without delay,' said Angus, 'for we need to be getting on with the repairs to that room.'

'Who are you hustling?' old Mr. Cameron shouted, shaking the stick. 'Get outa here, the lot of you. Send that fellah Moore in here. Hi you, Macdonald, come back here. I want to talk to you. I been wanting to talk to you this two weeks. First time I ever waited so long to talk to anybody. Shona!' he called as the rest of us were going out, and I went back. 'You just about made me the happiest fellah in the world. Good night.'

The next morning, breakfast was taken to his room at seven, and by eight he was sitting in the car in the courtyard, asking whether we were all coming to Strathdonan that morning or next week, so, in the end, we all piled into the cars with pieces of toast and marmalade in our hands and drove away. In the village, Findlay was standing at his garden gate, so Aunt stopped, called to Mrs. Elton: 'We've got a picnic lunch,' and Findlay came in with Neil, Donald and me.

At Strathdonan not only the joiners and other workmen were there, but also a crowd of other people like Kenny the Shepherd and Robbie the Forester, who had all come to see the gravestones. Aunt shepherded the Camerons from Canada into the room first and showed them the stone and, in spite of the crowd of excited people, it was as quiet as in church while old Mr. Cameron stood looking down and reading the names: '"Evan Cameron, Stone Mason. Mary Cameron, widow of Evan Cameron—"'

'It has occurred to me,' Aunt said very quietly, 'that these stones having been brought here between 1804 and 1810 is providential. If they had been exposed untended to the weather until now, the names would all have been worn away.'

'Maybe you've got something there,' old Mr. Cameron said quietly and then his voice took on its usual impatient tone, 'but right now they are going back where they belong and I'll see that they're looked after so that the names don't wear away.' He turned to Somerled. 'Okay, get going. Pick 'em up and load them on that trailer outside.'

With all of us working and with two tractors and trailers shuttling to and fro up the glen to the graveyard, it took us until four in the afternoon to get all those gravestones out, for there were three layers of them, with layers of sand in between and, as Angus had prophesied, the stone of Davie Farquhar's family was in the bottom layer. When we stopped to have a cup of tea, I could feel the sand in my ears and among my hair, and we all smelled of rotten wood; but the house felt happier than it had ever felt before, although the drawing-room was a shambles with the door opening into what looked like a wet sandpit.

'Let's give it best for today,' Somerled said, looking down into the soggy mess. 'We'll need all the men to have that sand out and we can't get them until the old emperor has got his graveyard fixed up. I say, let's all go up there!'

And so, towards six o'clock we all arrived at the grave-yard, but without Findlay, who suddenly decided that he was going home. We went in the Land-Rover and behind came Young Kenny with the tractor and trailer loaded with the joiners and people, and everybody was whistling and singing. The first time I saw this place was when Aunt took

my brothers and me to visit Angus for the first time and
then the track had been only a footpath. Now there was a
broad track made by the lorries bringing in the stone for
Mr. Cameron's wall. Then, the last time I had been here,
there had been only some bits of wall, but, now, Jamie the
Blacksmith's beautiful wrought-iron gates had been hung
and already most of the gravestones were in place, all round
the inside of the wall, with an open green place in the
middle. It looked beautiful and, although it was a graveyard,
it had the effect of bringing the whole Broad Glen to life, for
these stones recalled the people who had once been born and
had then lived and worked and eventually died in this place.

Proudly, old Mr. Cameron led us round the rectangle and
everybody was quiet now. These old gravestones were not
made to stand up but to lie flat on the ground, and as we
walked round, people tended to stop at the stone that bore
their own names and soon the whole green rectangle was
dotted with little groups of people.

'I would like, if it's possible,' old Mr. Cameron said, 'to
have some man of the church bless this place. You could
arrange that, young fellah?'

'Easily, sir,' Somerled said. 'When would you like it to be?'

'There's no rush,' said old Mr. Cameron for once. 'Say we make it the last Sunday before I go back to Toronto? I'd like to remember a service in this place,' he said quietly. 'You sure you got all the stones out of that hole?' he asked then.

'I think so, sir. We seem to be left with nothing but a sandy swamp.'

'Told you there was a swamp in there, Shona,' old Mr. Cameron said to me.

It was just as well that there were no special guests arriving at the hotel these days, because we had all become so enthusiastic about Strathdonan that we forgot our duties as hotel-keepers. It was adventurous, digging about in that mess of soggy sand, for, after finding the gravestones one could not escape the idea that one might find something else, and on the next day we all dug down and down until, just after lunch, Somerled said to the master mason: 'Sinclair, this is ridiculous. In the middle here we are nearly six feet down. There is something very odd about this.'

Mr. Sinclair jumped into the hole and began to scrape sand away from one side with a shovel.

'It's an odd bit of building,' he said. 'This wall below the floor level is far older than what's up above. They must have used an old wall for the foundation of this new wing.'

'Wait a minute,' said Aunt. 'You go up steps to go into the old house. It is possible there was another door on this side with steps going down to a courtyard or something. What about concentrating the digging at the end nearest the old house to see what we find?'

Until now, we had been digging in the middle, trying to see how deep we could get, but now we all moved along, a row of us across the width of the room and we began to clear the place methodically. It seemed to me that we might go on shovelling for ever as we moved, digging, towards the end of the room and then went back and moved up again, taking away another layer of sand as we came, but, at last, there was a clonking sound and the man whose shovel had made the noise shouted: 'Gold, boys!'

We all stood watching while three men scraped and prodded and shovelled very carefully now and soon an old stone step, worn down into a hollow in the middle, came into sight and underneath it another and another until there were five steps altogether. Mr. Sinclair got down on his knees at the bottom of them and brushed some sand away with his hands before he looked up and said: 'We're down to the level. These are cobblestones now,' and as he spoke a little trickle of water oozed along like a little snake between the egg-shaped cobbles.

'It's the old well yard!' Aunt said loudly, and Somerled and all the men looked at her as if she were dotty.

'Are you demented, Liz?' Somerled asked. 'Who would build over a rising well?'

'Gordon the Gambler did,' said Aunt. 'What will you bet? It's pretty silly, I admit, but I suppose he thought he could keep the water down with sand and gravestones and he was trying to build a grand house on the cheap. Now, you young people, dig only where Mr. Sinclair says. We don't want to have to fish you out of a well.'

I came up the ramp and out of the hole altogether now and sat on the edge with Aunt and Angus, but Neil, Donald and Findlay went on burrowing like terriers until suddenly Findlay stood up straight in the corner that Mr. Sinclair had given them to dig and said: 'Angus!' while he pointed at his feet.

'Aunt,' said Neil, 'it's a man's face on a stone! A man with whiskers!'

'Camerons calling and repeating,' said Donald, 'whiskers!'

'Ow!' I yelped, for Aunt had taken such a grip on my arm that I thought it was going to break.

'Sorry, Shona,' she said, scrambling to her feet and down the ramp into the hole.

She looked down at Findlay's 'Angus,' the man with the whiskers, then knelt down and began to push the sand away from around the carved, bearded face until we could all see the circle of the carved halo round the head. She looked up at Mr. Sinclair, her dirty hands clasped in front of her as if she were kneeling there, praying. 'Oh, Sinclair,' she said, 'be careful. Somerled, be careful. It is part of the Strathdonan Stone. Maybe the whole stone is here.'

Her voice was all shaky, but suddenly it changed and she became like the police sergeant, as Angus calls it. 'Neil, Donald, get up out of here and take Findlay with you. And the rest of you, no shovels. Use your hands.'

She stayed down there while we all sat with Angus and bit by bit the great stone came into sight. Soon we could see the rounded top of it and the carved, bearded heads of the two men on the face and then, inch by inch, the length of it was cleared until we could see the long, carved squiggles of the endless snake-like pattern that is characteristic of Early Celtic sculpture. As each little bit came into sight, Aunt would make a noise like a sob before she began to push and brush at the sand again, and when, at last, it was all exposed, she said: 'Heavens, what a beauty! And not a crack in the whole length of it.'

'Seven feet, eight inches and three-quarters, not counting the bit that goes below ground,' said Somerled, kneeling beside it with a foot-rule, 'by four feet one and a half inches wide. Pity it is so big, Liz. I'd have given it to you for a locket!'

'Silly ass,' she said, blinking her eyes as if she were crying and then: 'Heavens, what a smell!' and, as she spoke, there came that eerie sob: 'Uh-uh-uh!' but louder than ever before, and a little jet of water came spouting up by the side of the great stone.

Aunt stood up, looked down at the stone and gave a long sigh. 'Gordon's men got it in here without breaking it over a hundred and fifty years ago,' she said, looking at Somerled. 'They believed probably that some terrible curse would befall them for moving it, but the curse would be more terrible still if they damaged it. We don't believe in curses any more, but, still, can we get this stone out of here without damaging it?'

'Of course we can, Liz!' said Somerled. 'We'll get those heavy-lift chaps we had for the repair of the Great Tower. They'll take it out through that window over there like a feather on the breeze. But where will we put it? Isn't it what Aunt Coocoo would call a-little-too-*large*-don't-you-think for the top of the piano?'

All the men laughed and Aunt smiled and looked away wistfully through the window, across the loch and on up to the top of the green hill on the other side, the hill to the south which she thought was the original site of the Strathdonan Stone.

'But we could never put it up there!' Somerled protested, reading her thoughts.

'What man has done, man can do,' said Angus suddenly in his quiet voice and we all looked at him. 'I do not know how the men of long ago put that stone on the hill where Elizabeth thinks it stood, but I think she is right in her belief that they did put it there. We can put it there, too, although by a different means, perhaps.'

'The big crawler tractor from the forestry plantation could take it!' said Neil.

Somerled shook his head. 'Not up that hill, Neil, with all the boulders and swampy bits.'

'Do you know the best way to find a safe track up a hill, Neil?' Angus asked.

'No.'

'You just watch the way the sheep go, man,' said Young Kenny, digging Neil in the ribs. 'Easy.'

'Young Kenny,' said Angus, 'do you know the best track to the top of the Green Hill there?'

'I wouldn't say for sure, Angus,' said Young Kenny cautiously.

'Would you follow *me* up the Green Hill with the big tractor and the Strathdonan Stone, Young Kenny?'

'Och aye, Angus, man,' said Young Kenny confidently. 'Surely.'

Angus looked at Somerled. 'Then, some fine day when it is convenient for us to have the big tractor and that contrivance you have for carrying the trees, Macdonald,' he said, 'Young Kenny and I will take the stone up the Green Hill, but some of the rest of you will have to come up and make a hole at the place and of the depth that Miss Cameron says, for I am a little older now and will not care to dig a hole after climbing that hill and Young Kenny cannot dig a hole whatever, having no notion of how to do anything except poach and drive tractors.'

Somerled looked down at the stone, then at Aunt, then at the top of the Green Hill, and last of all at Angus. Then he smiled. 'You and Young Kenny can have the big crawler any day you want it,' he said.

11. *Going Home*

THE men from Rioch who specialised in the repair of old
buildings built of huge stones, buildings like Castle
Vannich, took the stone out of its hole under the floor, and
then through a window that had all its glass and its frame
removed, like a feather on the breeze, as Somerled had said.
But it was no feather. It was a pillar, really, roughly square
and measuring about four feet on every side and all the
sides were carved, but the first side we had seen was more
decorated than the others and only this side had the faces of
the two bearded men, who, Aunt said, were probably meant
to be St. Donan and one of his disciples. Wrapped in heavy
bandages of sacking to protect it from the six great chains
that were round it, it was laid on the trailer that carried the
tree trunks from the forest, and then the foreman of the
squad from Rioch said: 'Okay, there she is, Macdonald.
Where do we go from here?'

With a grin, Somerled swung round and pointed away
to the top of the Green Hill. 'Up to the summit there,' he
said.

At first, the man thought that Somerled was joking, but when he realised he was not, he said: 'You'll have to count us out, Macdonald. We could never get our lifting gear away up there. I don't know of any firm in the north here who would do it, either. I don't know of a firm that would try to take the *stone* up there, even, among all those swamps and rocks.'

'We've got a firm right here who will take it up,' Aunt said, and the man stared at her as she went on: 'If *we* put the stone on the hilltop, will *you* tell us the easiest way to set it up vertically when we get it there?'

The man looked from Aunt to Somerled, then from the top of the hill to the stone on the trailer and then he took off his cap, scratched his head, put the cap back on and said to his second-in-command: 'It could be done with a tripod frame, a hand tackle and the Devil's own luck, maybe.'

'You supply the frame and tackle and we'll see to the luck,' Somerled said. 'Which day can you come?'

'Hold on a minute, Macdonald,' Angus said in his quiet way that yet drew the attention of everybody. 'There is a change in the weather, I am thinking. It is turning to rain. Young Kenny and I are not going to set off with the stone unless the hill is dry. There is a bad bit of wet moss on the west shoulder.' He turned to the foreman. 'If the Macdonald was to telephone you the evening before we wanted you, would you be able to come at short notice?'

The man smiled. 'To see this ploy, myself and Willie here will be with you inside five minutes.' He jerked his head at the trailer. 'We've moved a thing or two in our time, but we would like to see that stone going up that hill.'

The foreman and Willie went away back to Rioch, and

it was all very flat and disappointing. Even as their lorry with the crane on it drove away, the first spots of rain began to fall, which is sort of typical of the North of Scotland. Always, it seems, when things are at their most exciting and you need good weather, the rain comes on. Neil, Donald and I had more or less thought that, as soon as we had the stone out in the open, we would all set off on a triumphant march behind Angus and Young Kenny with the tractor up the Green Hill, where the huge hole in which the stone was to stand had already been dug, but now our spirits went right down to the bottom of the smelly old well that the stone had been covering.

Until this time, that summer, the weather had been un-usually good, and, as Aunt pointed out, anyone who expects a perfect August as well as a perfect July in the Highlands is expectant to the point of idiocy, so there it was. The stone lay in its bandages on the trailer and we could not see the Green Hill across the loch through the sheets of rain.

It rained and it rained and it rained. Some days, it was dry in the forenoon, but, during lunch, it would start to pour again, and other days it would rain all forenoon and dry up in the afternoon, but, from Strathdonan, you could see, during the dry periods, little silver streams tumbling down the side of the Green Hill into the loch and it looked more and more impossible that the tractor with the stone would ever get up there at all, in spite of Angus telling us that the steep slopes would drain quickly and the stream courses become tiny trickles very shortly after the rain stopped.

On the second-last Sunday of the holidays, we had the service for the blessing of old Mr. Cameron's graveyard and the rain stayed off for just long enough, and no more. All the people from the hotel and the village and all round about came winding along the track from the fork, where all the cars except the Land-Rovers had to be left, and it was as if history had turned back for an afternoon when the huge crowd had gathered round the old church, as the people of the Glen used to do, long ago, in the days before the Clearance. While the minister, standing in the centre of the graveyard, spoke of the people who had once lived here and who were buried under this green grass, I looked up at Ben Vannich and saw that the clouds had rolled away from it, as if it, too, had come out to attend the service, but as the final prayer was being said, the clouds rolled down again, Ben Vannich disappeared, and before we had walked back to the fork, it was raining again as if it had never rained before.

That evening, though, Angus sniffed the air and then looked up at the blue banner with the White Hind on it that flew from the Great Tower of the castle. The banner, which, for two weeks, had been whipping in the south-west wind so that the White Hind seemed to be in full flight from the lashing rain, was now hanging limp against the flagstaff, not moving at all.

'The weather is making a change, I am thinking,' Angus said. He is an absolute wizard about the weather and, in spite of the fact that the rain was still pouring down, I felt as I looked up that my spirits were rising as high as the banner on the Great Tower.

'If we get a puff of wind from due west or a little north of it, it will dry that Green Hill in no time,' he said, looking up at the banner again.

I looked up, too, and saw the corner of it lift a little, fall back against the pole and then take heart and lift again, and before bedtime it was blowing straight out on a westerly wind, high above but parallel with the roof of the south front.

'There she goes,' said Angus. 'We will get your stone home this summer yet, Elizabeth.'

The next morning, Neil, Donald and I came down, all ready to climb to the top of the Green Hill, but Angus merely shook his head and looked up at the White Hind sailing above the roof. 'That hill will need a little more of this wind before we tackle it,' he said.

The next day, the west wind was still blowing, but the thought of the stone and the Green Hill was put out of all our heads at breakfast by a sudden fracas breaking out at the table where the Camerons from Canada sat. Old Mr. Cameron was having breakfast in the dining-room for once and all the guests were startled when he suddenly jumped out of his chair, banged his stick on the floor and shouted: 'You stop mollycoddlin' me like I was helpless! I'm not goin', I tell you. I'm stayin' right here at home in Vannich!' He then set off in his determined jerky way towards the door, with all his family rushing behind him, protesting, while he marched on, taking no notice, and then Mr. Fourth left the procession, came over to our table and slumped into a chair.

'Dad has decided he is not going to leave tomorrow,' he told Aunt.

'Not leave?'

'He wants to see the Strathdonan Stone set up. He wants to supervise the Strathdonan development. He wants to do a million things around here and he wants to retain his suite for the winter, along with the rooms for Scott and Moore.'

M

He sighed. 'Is there anybody can tell me what you *do* with a man like Dad?' he asked, looking round at us.

'I do not see that you have to do anything with the old gentleman,' Angus said quietly, 'for he seems to know very well what he wants to do with himself. Why should he not stay at home here instead of going back to Toronto?' Mr. Fourth and all of us stared at him and he went on: 'The Glen of Vannich takes a strong hold on its people and your father feels that grip. You are worried about his health, I know, but it is my belief that he will live longer here in Vannich than in any other place on earth.'

'Angus may be right, Mr. Fourth,' Aunt said.

'And in these days of flying machines,' Angus continued, 'you can come to visit him at any time. Do not be worrying yourself about the old gentleman. All of us here will keep an eye on him and myself will be very pleased to have the company of somebody who is a little like my own age.'

Angus rose from the table and went away as if nothing unusual had happened, and, somehow, the matter was settled right there.

The next day, Mr. and Mrs. Fourth, Fifth, a secretary and a chauffeur drove away while old Mr. Cameron shook his stick at the departing car and shouted: 'Remember what I said about that Vancouver contract. Any trouble, put 'em on to *me*!' and then, as if nothing strange had happened, as if his whole family had not just left for the other side of the world, he turned to Angus and said: 'Look here, when we goin' to get that stone up that hill?'

We all looked up at the banner on the tower, where the White Hind still galloped eastwards in front of the westerly wind, and Angus said: 'By this evening, we may be able to decide. In the meantime, I have had a small idea about that boy Findlay.'

'What, Angus?' Aunt asked.

Angus looked at old Mr. Cameron before he said: 'Now that we have this gentleman in our midst for good, we must get Findlay accustomed to that stick and I think that the best way to do it may be to make sticks the fashion.'

'The fashion?' Aunt repeated.

'Yes. Fashion is a very peculiar thing. People will get used to anything if it is the fashion. As you know, I amuse myself now and then with the carving of crooks and sticks, but, like Miss Dorothy and Miss Constance, I have no liking for selling things. However, I would like to give all of you a present of a stick, which you will find useful when we climb the Green Hill and we will give one to Findlay, too, if we can persuade him to take it.'

We went with Angus straight away and were allowed to choose our sticks. Mine is a miniature shepherd's crook with a ram's-horn handle that ends in a tiny carved ram's head, and Neil and Donald chose crooks taller than themselves, and then Aunt went off to the village to fetch Findlay. Angus picked out from his collection another crook, a very beautiful one, a little taller than Neil's and we all came out into the courtyard, where he stood it against the Stirrup Stone to await Findlay's coming.

'What goes on?' Somerled asked, coming to join us.

When we told him of our plan, he went indoors and fetched his own great tall crook which made all of ours look like matchsticks.

'Young Kenny is coming on quite well at the piping,' Angus said now, cocking his ear towards the blacksmith's shop from where we could hear the sound of bagpipes being tuned. 'He has a very fine ear. That boy is good for nothing but poaching and piping and tractor-driving and wasting his time, as they call it. He is a proper Highlandman and a fine thing, too, for there are not many of us left that specialise in being happy. Run over there, Neil, and tell him to come out and give us a tune.'

Young Kenny came marching out of the blacksmith's shop to the tune of 'The Macdonald's Return to Vannich' and Somerled said to Neil and Donald: 'I bet you can't do this!' and he began to march in front of Young Kenny, using his tall crook like a drum-major's staff, spinning it round his fingers, then throwing it, twirling, into the air and catching it, all in time with the beat of the music. It all looked terribly easy, but when Neil, Donald and I tried to do it, our sticks went flying in all directions until Angus said that if Findlay arrived and saw all these sticks hurtling about, our whole plan would be a failure.

When the car came, we all stood leaning on our sticks like old Mr. Cameron, but Findlay, who had opened the door ready to jump out, slammed it shut again and shrank as close as he could get against Aunt. I picked up his own crook from the Stirrup Stone, held it up and said: 'Look, Findlay, this is for you,' but his eyes became wide with terror and he cringed down in his seat.

'Play a tune for Findlay, Young Kenny,' Angus said, throwing his own crook out of sight behind the Stirrup Stone, and all of us, including old Mr. Cameron, hid our sticks away, too.

Young Kenny began to play a march and, like all real pipers when they play in march-time, began to march away across the courtyard, and Findlay, after a little while, sat up in his car seat and began to smile as he listened to the

music. Suddenly I discovered that Somerled was away at
the far end of the courtyard with Young Kenny and he
began to do his clowning drum-major act with his tall crook.
A lot of the guests came out of the hotel to listen and to
watch, and it was odd to realise that they all thought we
were simply having fun and that none of them knew that
this was a tremendous effort to cure Findlay of his terror of
a walking-stick of any kind.

When Young Kenny stopped playing to catch his breath,
all the spectators applauded and Findlay clapped his hands,
too, and then jumped out of the car. Somerled pointed to
our sticks that were lying behind the Stirrup Stone and called
us all down to the far end of the courtyard, where we went,
carrying the sticks in front of us so that Findlay could not
see them.

'We'll march up and down here,' Somerled said. 'The
rest of you simply use your sticks like walking-sticks or
wave them about if you like, but don't let them drop or get
out of control.'

Young Kenny began to play, and Mr. Cameron, Angus,
Neil, Donald and I fell in behind him and Somerled, and
marched to and fro, but not going near Findlay. At first,
he clung close to Aunt, holding on to her hand, but quite
soon he began to smile, and when Somerled threw his crook
high into the air, where it whirled over and over, he watched
it fearfully at first, but then gave a shout of pleasure when
Somerled caught it and went marching on. After a little, I
realised that Somerled was leading us nearer and nearer to
Aunt and Findlay and, quite soon, only the Stirrup Stone
was between us, while Somerled's crook went up into the
air and was caught again and again. Suddenly, Findlay saw
the stick that Angus had placed against the Stirrup Stone,

broke away from Aunt, seized it and tossed it into the air in imitation of Somerled. We all stood dead still and Kenny's pipes gave a funny off-tune squeak as we watched Findlay's stick.

'Keep playing, man!' said Somerled urgently, and the pipes came into tune again as the stick came down and Findlay caught it deftly and went marching away with it across the courtyard, stamping it into the gravel in time to the music, imitating Somerled again.

With long strides, Somerled and Young Kenny caught up with him and fell in behind, and the rest of us hustled into line and marched right round the big rectangle until we came back to the Stirrup Stone, where Somerled said: 'Up, Findlay, boy,' and prodded him gently from behind, so that he went up the three stone steps and on to the platform. 'Up she goes!' Somerled shouted, and tossed up his crook, and Findlay threw his up, too, and, as they caught them, Young Kenny stopped playing. All the people round about, who thought we had been trying to entertain them, began to applaud wildly and shout: 'Encore!' and Findlay, feeling that he had made all these people happy, smiled round and waved his stick delightedly until, suddenly overcome by shyness, he jumped down from his platform and ran to Aunt. But he did not drop his stick. He began to show it to Aunt, pointing out to her the carved eagle on its handle.

'Yes, Findlay,' she said. 'It is beautiful.' She took her own stick out of the back of the car. 'This is mine, but it is not so handsome as yours.'

He now came round us all, examining our sticks, but when he took old Mr. Cameron's, the one which had frightened him so much, a stick of plain black ebony with a gold band, he shook his head sadly and sighed as he handed it back, as if to say that, as sticks went, this one was a very poor affair. The people round about were still calling to us and asking for more music, and they did not seem to see that Aunt was all trembly and nearly in tears with sheer joy or that the rest of us were bursting with triumph at this great victory we had won, so it was a relief when Somerled said: 'All right, fall in, the comic army, and we'll go round the courtyard once more. Ready, Findlay?' Holding his crook by its point against his chest, Somerled stood to attention and Findlay did the same. 'One, two!' said Somerled and off we went, tramp, tramp round the courtyard again. It was really a march of victory, although the spectators did not know it.

The next day, my brothers and I got up early again, and the White Hind was still galloping in front of the wind, but, once again, Angus merely shook his head, so Aunt drove us down to Findlay's house, where the three of us spent most of the day trying to twiddle our sticks round our fingers as Somerled could do and as Findlay had learned to do without any trouble, but Neil, Donald and I were simply hopeless at it. However, after dinner that evening, we all went out into the courtyard, and Angus said: 'Those that want to see the stone reach its home should be on top of the Green Hill at midday tomorrow. The hill may still be a little damp, but if we wait any longer, it may be damper still, I am thinking.'

Angus and Somerled went away to Strathdonan to spend the night, for they, with Young Kenny, the tractor and a team of men intended to leave for the Green Hill at dawn. Neil and Donald, of course, wanted to go with them, but Aunt turned into the police sergeant and sent us all to bed at nine o'clock instead.

'You have no conception of the distance they will cover before they get that tractor up there,' she told Neil. 'They will weave to and fro around that hill for miles and how Angus can tackle it at all at his age I don't know.'

'What age is he?' one of us asked for maybe the hundredth time.

'I don't know, but he is still young enough to do what none of the rest of us can do, which is to lead that stone up that hill.'

I woke up at six the next morning and went into the boys' room, for there was no point in letting them start the day badly by hopping about and disturbing Aunt before it was time, but I had not been in there for five minutes when she appeared, fully dressed. 'Breakfast in quarter of an hour,' she said. 'I am going down to put the food in the car. Bring your haversacks.'

We were at Strathdonan by eight o'clock, and the whole village and all the people round about—men, women and children—were there, too, sitting on the shore of the loch in the early sun. Aunt began to distribute the food out of the car into the gamekeeper's bags and the haversacks of the people who were going to climb the hill, and Kenny the Shepherd came forward with Findlay and said: 'Put a little extra in our bags, for we are two hungry sort of fellows, my friend Findlay and me.' And then there was a sudden shout from the lochside: 'Look! She's coming round the hill!' Aunt whipped out her field-glasses, but without glasses I could see the big yellow tractor with the trailer behind, Angus and Somerled walking in front of it and a stream of men walking behind it, while the Land-Rover, with old Mr. Cameron, Miss Dotty and Miss Coocoo, brought up the rear. The whole procession, moving along the

face of the hill, looked like a caterpillar on a cabbage
leaf.

And now we all piled into the trailers that would take us
as far up the hill as they could go, and all the people left
beside the loch cheered as we drove away. But the trailers
did not take us very far in a going-up direction. They stopped
among a lot of huge boulders and we all got down and
looked at this green slope with patches of heather here and
there rising above us and Kenny the Shepherd pointed with
his crook and said: 'That tractor hadn't much room to spare
getting through between these two rocks.' It was only then
that I noticed the marks of the heavy tractor on the grass
and Neil and Donald, with a whoop, set out to follow the
marks.

'Come back here, you two,' Aunt called. 'Kenny will take
us up by a shorter way.'

'I wouldn't take the stone up like Angus,' Kenny said,
'but if you will all follow me I will take *you* up without
losing all the wind that is in you.'

I soon began to feel that Kenny the Shepherd had a very
high opinion of my wind, for I seemed to have lost it all in
the first five minutes, and that green slope kept rising in front
of us. Each time we came to a crest which I thought was the
top I found myself in another wrinkle of the hill with
another green slope rising until I got to the stage of not
looking up at all, but down at Aunt's heels, which were
plod-plodding along in front of me until suddenly she sat
down, saying: 'In the words of Angus, Kenny, I am not
so good at the climbing since I got a little older and this hill
twice in one fortnight is nearly too much,' and I discovered
that we were at the top, beside a big hole in the ground and
a pile of earth and stones.

Away to our left, I could see Ben Vannich, and beyond its left shoulder lay Loch Vannich and the castle. To our right the hills that surrounded Strathdonan flattened away towards the North Sea, which was hidden in summer mist, and down below lay the house of Strathdonan, on the other side of the little loch, which reflected the grey sunlit walls. The crowd of people between the house and the loch looked like a swarm of ants.

Nobody on the top of the hill spoke very much. We were all too busy listening for the throb of the tractor's engine, which now seemed quite near and then a long way off. And sometimes there would be dead silence and we would all be tense, wondering if something had gone wrong, until we heard the beat of the engine again. We all jumped when Kenny the Shepherd said: 'That's her about to start on the last rise. I will go to meet her, but it will be safer if the rest of you will stay here. There is not much room. She will come on to the top here from the east there, by the side of that boulder.'

Aunt became very police sergeant when Kenny had disappeared down the slope and would not let anybody move and it seemed like ages before Kenny and Somerled and Angus appeared, then Young Kenny perched on the huge tractor like a sparrow on a roof-top and then the stone, lying on the long trailer, surrounded by the group of men. As the Land-Rover came into sight, Young Kenny shut off the tractor engine and there was a moment of dead silence before, as if it had been prearranged, but it was not, we all began to cheer and shout as if we had gone crazy, and the people down below by the loch were cheering and shouting, too.

Sacks of sand and cement and an oil-drum full of water

had come up the hill with the stone and Somerled and some of the men fell to with shovels and mixed a heap of cement.

'Now for it,' Somerled said when they had thrown some cement into the hole. He looked at the foreman and Willie. 'Over to you two. You tell the rest of us what to do and we'll try to do it. The carved face of the stone should face north over Strathdonan.'

The two men set up a tall tripod of steel which had a block and tackle at the top over the hole and then Young Kenny manœuvred the trailer with the stone into exactly the position they wanted, with the bottom of the stone nearest to the hole in the ground. Then they fixed steel ropes to all the sacking and chain bandages and ten men were given numbers and the end of a rope each.

'When I call "Ten," Macdonald,' the foreman said, 'take a strong, steady pull on your rope till I shout "Stop." The same goes for all you others. Don't move unless your numbers are called.'

'Shona, come on the end of this rope and give a hand,' Somerled said, 'and Aunt Dotty and Aunt Coocoo, get in behind Shona,' and in the end all of us except Angus and old Mr. Cameron were attached to the ropes and spread out at the ends of them round the whole top of the hill, so that we looked like a huge spider, of which the stone was the body. The foreman looked round at us all, took off his cap, scratched his head and put the cap back on before he said gravely: 'Now, all joking apart, I am not keen on this. We haven't enough working room up here and we have no control over that stone except these ropes and you people and my eye watching the base.'

'If it's sharp eyes you want,' Somerled said, 'you've got two good pairs that you're not using. Mr. Cameron and

Angus, get round the north side there and watch the base for us and yell the minute it goes out of line.'

We all became very tense as Willie began to pull on the chain of the tackle and very slowly, but steadily, the head of the great stone began to rise, and when the foreman called: 'Ten, nine, eight, seven!' I was so busy watching the great weight moving that I forgot to pull until I saw Somerled's shoulders pulling back towards me. 'Stop!' the foreman said sharply, and then Willie on the tackle raised the head of the stone another few inches. It went on like this for what seemed to be a very long time, with everybody very alert and very tense, and the calling of the numbers came more and more rapidly and more and more sharply until, with the stone hanging half in mid-air, half resting on the trailer, the foreman came and re-positioned us all at the ends of our ropes.

'At the next pull on the tackle,' he told Somerled and us and Kenny the Shepherd and Aunt and Findlay, who were Number Nine, 'she will tip, and Ten and Nine will have to jump to it. If she slews, we may miss the hole, so at the first shout, pull with all you've got. It'd be a pity to let her roll down the hill again at this stage.'

I took such a grip on that rope that my hands ached for days afterwards, because I could not bear anything to go wrong now, and when the tackle began to creak, I could hardly breathe. There was a sudden shout from Angus of 'Macdonald!' and of 'Ten!' from the foreman. Somerled's shoulders came back, and I staggered back, pulling behind him and then there was a terrific thud, then a shriek from Miss Coocoo and I shut my eyes, waiting to be crushed to death by the Strathdonan Stone, but all that happened was Angus's quiet voice saying: 'Well done, the lot of you. She

is right home. My, is that not a bonnie sight!' I opened
my eyes and there was the empty trailer and the stone standing upright on its hilltop, and the foreman was mopping
his forehead as he said: 'By Jove, that was touch and go
for a second!' Somerled let go of the rope and looked at
his watch. 'It was a roundabout road for a short cut that
you led us, Angus, but it was a safe one,' he said. 'Seven
hours it has taken us, but the stone is here, Liz. It is five to
one.'

A faint noise of cheering was rising from the crowd beside the loch away down below and, looking down, I saw a shadow on the water that extended across and ended on the roof the house.

'Up here,' Angus said, 'there is no time of the clock, Macdonald,' and, looking away down over the loch and the strath, he quoted:

' " It is the bright of the day when the saints bless
      Strathdonan

    And rest on the house in the shade of their Stone—" '
and, suddenly, everybody was singing:

' She is the peace of the night when the moon lights
      Strathdonan
And the saint raise their prayers to God on His throne.'

The men made more cement, throwing it into the deep hole and all the rest of us collected the biggest boulders we could carry and threw them in among the cement while the foreman kept checking with a spirit-level to make sure that the stone was dead upright.

When the hole was full, we put back the clods of green turf that had been lifted, and when we had finished you would never have known that the stone had ever been moved or had spent over a hundred and fifty years under the house in the strath down below.

'I am so hungry,' Kenny the Shepherd said then, 'that I could eat a horse. Findlay, where is that bag?'

All the rest of us suddenly discovered that we were hungry, too, not having had our usual elevenses or anything, with all the excitement, and Aunt was worrying in case there might not be enough food, when Miss Dotty and Miss Coocoo astounded us all by producing a huge hamper from the back of the Land-Rover.

'We brought it because we felt we should stay with the *Saints* for a little while, don't you know,' Miss Coocoo explained. 'It must be so strange for them to come out into the world again, poor things, don't you think? What in the *world* is that clumsy-looking grey building away over there?'

'Castle Vannich,' Aunt said.

'How *very* odd! Things look so different when you are up above *them* instead of they being up above *you*, if you see what I mean. Dotty, isn't it *quite* hideous?'

'Utterly,' said Miss Dotty, unwrapping a leg of roast mutton, looking at it with disgust and then handing it, paper and all, to the foreman from Rioch.

We sat eating for a very long time and then Miss Coocoo produced Young Kenny's pipes from the Land-Rover and we did some marching and stick-twiddling round the stone until we made ourselves hungry again, and then we sat down and ate some more until the wind, which had been warm in the bright sunshine, suddenly changed direction and became quite cold. Angus rose to his feet and stood looking down over the loch, where a faint ghostly mist was beginning to move over the water from the east.

'It will come to rain again before morning,' he said, 'but we have had a beautiful day and we are thankful for it and for the work we have done.' He paused for a moment and it was as if he had said a prayer. Then he went on: 'It is time that we went now, though. The evening mist is coming along the strath.'

We began to pack up, which did not take long, and soon the tractor and trailer and the Land-Rover set off on their long way down the hill, following their own tracks, and Angus rode away with Mr. Cameron, Miss Dotty and Miss Coocoo, but Somerled walked down the short way with the rest of us.

As we walked, we sang the Song of Strathdonan again, and I like the last verse best of all, because, while the others sang it, I watched the mist rolling over the strath down below and it was as if the earth were withdrawing into sleep, and I felt the beautiful peace that the song describes.

And have you seen evening come down on Strathdonan,
When the mist fills the valley like rolling sea foam?
My love is the peace that comes then to Strathdonan,
The peace of the darkening when tired men go home.

PRINTED IN GREAT BRITAIN BY
NORTHUMBERLAND PRESS LIMITED
GATESHEAD